MRS. DARLING'S DAUGHTER

Mrs. Darling's Daughter

by Hila Colman

WILLIAM MORROW & COMPANY
New York, 1962

MRS. DARLING'S DAUGHTER

Chapter 1

FROM the screened porch Victoria could hear her mother's voice speaking on the telephone. It was a clear, rather pretty voice that every once in a while trailed off on a high note and broke into a little squeal of laughter. It was precisely those high notes and the accompanying laughter that grated on Victoria's nerves. The word *gushing* entered her mind, and as her eyes swept over the lawn and stopped at her mother's carefully arranged flower beds, green with their early spring buds, she had a wild desire to open her mouth and scream.

"I do think gladioli are just a wee bit funereal, don't you?" her mother was saying in her most coaxing tone. "Don't you think white phlox would be nice, with perhaps a touch of larkspur? We could do the whole thing in blue and white, wouldn't it be fun?" Her voice

9

ended up high, and the little laugh followed. "A white cake with blue candles, and tie the presents in blue ribbon. Oh, I do believe that color scheme would be sweet. . . ."

When her mother finally hung up the phone and came out on the porch, Victoria controlled her feelings and eyed her quite calmly. "What's this all about? You've been on the phone all morning!"

"Have I, darling?" Her mother's blue eyes were innocent. "There's so much to do. It's the party we're giving for dear old Mrs. Honeycomb. She's going to be eighty, poor dear."

"Why are *you* giving the party?" asked Victoria. "What is old Mrs. Honeycomb to you? Why are you always organizing something?" Victoria stared at her mother as if she were a stranger.

Mrs. Darling looked hurt. "But Tory, dear, I like to do things for people, and I do think I can be helpful. They were going to fix up the library as if it were poor Mrs. Honeycomb's funeral, not her birthday party. All purple ribbons and gladioli!" Mrs. Darling wrinkled up her nose into a grimace. "What are you doing, dear?" She looked at her daughter sprawled across a long, low canvas chair. "You've been sitting here all morning," she added accusingly. "I don't know how you can just sit and do nothing."

"I can do it very easily," Tory said matter-of-factly.

"This is my vacation, and I shall probably spend a good deal of it doing what you call nothing."

Mrs. Darling looked at her daughter anxiously. "You're not worried about anything, are you, dear? You've been so touchy lately. You can confide in me."

"I'm fine. I just feel like sitting."

"Of course, dear. Well, *I* have a lot to do. Oh dear, it's after noon and this is my day at the hospital, and then I have to help decorate the library for Mrs. Honeycomb's party. . . ." Mrs. Darling hurried back into the house and left Tory to her sitting.

Tory let the magazine lying open across her lap slip off onto the porch floor. The cover displayed a smiling girl with very white teeth, standing on the deck of a ship waving good-by to a shadowy group below. The girl was very smartly dressed in a honey beige suit and a tiny pillbox hat. She had a corsage of orchids pinned onto her lapel. Sketched in lightly behind her was the silhouette of a young man, presumably her husband, since the caption said they were off on their honeymoon. Tory found herself staring at the girl and speculating on her life: she'll come home and be a pillar of the community, Tory decided; she'll join the church choir, help the Ladies' Aid, eventually be a secretary to the P.T.A., and a leader of a 4H group; in the evenings she will take adult education courses, she'll study

French and make little mushroom salt cellars in plastic molds.

I hate her, Tory thought, somewhat unnerved by the intensity of her own feelings. Why should she feel so strongly about a cover girl on a magazine, a stranger whom she didn't know?

Tory continued to sit and meditate while her mother fussed about the kitchen, probably eating her lunch. Later she heard her mother go upstairs, undoubtedly for her hat, bag, and gloves, and finally Tory heard her come back downstairs and go into the garage. Waving good-by, she watched her mother's tiny blue car pull out of the graveled driveway, turn the corner, and disappear from sight.

The house was marvelously quiet. Ethan, Tory's younger brother, had gone off early in the morning to a friend's house, and would not be home until suppertime. Tory slowly felt life returning to her body; she stretched herself and stood up. She didn't really feel like sitting; she felt a surging, restless, tremendous wave of energy that immobilized her because she didn't know what to do with it.

The truth was, Tory had a great longing for . . . she knew not what. Could a person long for something and not know what it was? Her best friend, Amy, said she wanted to fall in love. But Tory thought people either fell in love or they didn't. Perhaps she was simply longing for something to change. She was living in the same house she had always lived in, a large, old-fashioned two-storied house on Birch Drive in Squash Hollow, Connecticut, with her mother and father and her brother Ethan. She had turned sixteen last February, was a junior at the consolidated high school, she had taken her junior college board exams, and when she graduated a year from June, she would go on to some good small college either in New England or the Middle West.

Tory dated several boys in the high school. Her most recent date had been Adam Hopkins, a tall, quiet, dark-eyed boy, who had moved into town only a few months before. Amy thought he was "a fascinating enigma," but Tory wanted to make sure he really liked her before she let herself admit how fascinating she thought he was.

It was spring vacation now, and ordinarily this would bring great joy to Tory. But the awful truth was that she was farther from being happy than she could ever remember. Everything had turned sour, and she didn't know why. Life had become an endless stretch of monotonous days, one following the other in a meaningless fashion, with nothing accomplished, nothing to look forward to, and each day a grinding, stupid dullness to be unhappily endured. Here was a whole afternoon stretching out ahead of her, and there was nothing that she wanted to do except be alone, and that was not something positive; it was an absence of motion.

She could call up Amy and suggest that they take their first swim of the season at the lake, for it was unusually warm, but her mind recoiled at each step of the way: digging up her bathing suit from wherever it was put last fall, walking to the bus, going into the bathhouse to get undressed, and finally being on the beach —for what? To see the same old faces, hear the same old talk as last year, walk on the rocky beach, swim out to the raft and back. They would get dried and dressed, take the bus back, probably stop at Clancy's for a soda. The very thought of Squash Hollow village on this sleepy spring afternoon filled Tory with such distaste that she felt weak. And there was a whole summer of this stretching ahead of her!

Tory went inside the house and let the screen door bang behind her. Perhaps if she ate she'd feel better. She went into the kitchen and fixed herself a chicken sandwich and a glass of milk. The afternoon sun was pouring in through the kitchen window, so Tory carried her lunch into the living room, which was cooler. She sat down on the sofa, put her plate and glass on her mother's mahogany coffee table, and with a magazine under her sneakers, rested her feet on the table's edge. Her eyes roamed around the room, going from the velvet chairs with their tiny satin pillows meticulously

perched in their centers, to a curio cabinet in the corner, where her mother kept her collection of antique
demitasse cups, which were her pride and joy.

With a cool detachment Tory decided this was probably the ugliest room she had ever been in, and with a
slight tremor she wondered, not for the first time in
recent months, whether her feelings for her mother
could be the source of her misery. Up until this winter
her mother had been her mother, as good as anyone
else's mother, and someone Tory assumed she loved
with all the proper respect and affection due her. But
somehow in the past few months her mother had started
getting on her nerves. She could be feeling fine, as she
had this morning when she'd settled down on the porch
to read quietly. Then she would hear her mother talking on the phone in that sweet, gushing way she had
with certain people, and this thing would build up in
her so that she wanted to scream or explode. And there
was no stopping it. Once it started, everything about
her mother annoyed her. The distaste and irritation she
felt now with all the fussy little details of the room
were unnerving.

As her eyes went from one piece of furniture to the
next, Tory wondered how her mother could ever have
bought such atrocities. Why did she want a rocker with
arms carved like swans, and silk lamp shades with
fringe on them, and a huge square sofa upholstered in

a chintz covered with dozens of little Japanese men carrying buckets of water across their shoulders? Where were they carrying them to?

Why had her parents ever bought this big, ugly, old-fashioned house and chosen to live in a town that was dead—where there was absolutely nothing to do? Perhaps, Tory decided, Squash Hollow was at the bottom of her misery, and not her mother at all. The truth was, the town was dead.

Of course, the Chamber of Commerce's booklet made it sound as if the town were humming with activity. There were the Boy Scouts and the Brownies, and the 4H Clubs, and the Sunday Nights for Young Adults, and the Grange, and Little League, and a couple of bowling teams, and all the things her mother belonged to, like the Squash Hollow Literary Club, and the P.T.A., and the Ladies' Hospital Aid, and the Church Auxiliary Society. But when you added it all up, what did you have?

A dead town.

If she wanted to slave for something, Tory thought, it wouldn't be for any of the things her mother worked for. They were all so trivial. She was willing to work, but it had to be for something vital, something exciting and important. She didn't want to make the world safe for the P.T.A., or decorate the library for Mrs. Honeycomb, or sell cookies for the Brownies.

She wanted . . . well, she didn't know what she wanted, but she knew that everything she *didn't* want was here in Squash Hollow and in this house.

With a sudden burst of energy Tory drank down the last of her milk and went up the stairs to her room. She was taken aback by the angry look on her face as she caught her reflection in the mirror. The angry young woman of Squash Hollow, she thought to herself wryly. Tory stood in front of the mirror and twisted her hair around her fingers, and then tried holding it up in various ways. She had shoulder length, very fine blond hair —baby hair her mother called it—and in warm weather it hung with no body to it. Tory used to like her hair (she had thought its very fineness more aristocratic than coarser hair), but now, along with everything else, she was bored with it. She was bored with the healthy appearance of her somewhat Slavic face with its high cheekbones and wide-set gray eyes, she was bored with her own vitality, carrying her energy around like a burden with no place to deposit it.

She wished she were fragile and delicate, but as she turned in disgust from the mirror to face the room, a new thought struck her: her bedroom was as ugly as the living room downstairs. This was her haven, her room, but what of her was in it? Why had she never noticed it before? She was thunderstruck.

The room was completely in keeping with the rest of

the house, a further reflection of her mother and her mother's taste, another example of her mother's impossible penchant for dressing things up. Tory stared at the pink, ruffled chintz skirt around the bed; at the organdy over pink silk skirt draped around the dressing table; at the four-poster bed with its beribboned canopy. Even the small, chintz wing chair had a ruffled bottom, and the white lamp beside it had a shade decorated with tiny pink velvet bows.

This room was a creation of her mother, done several years before to satisfy her ideal of what a young girl's room should be. Tory felt a pulse throbbing in her temple. She felt as if she might be Alice in Wonderland with the room getting smaller and smaller and herself getting bigger and bigger. Actually she had outgrown this room ages ago and had never realized it until this minute!

With swift, energetic motions, Tory ripped the pink chintz skirt off the bed. It had rather nice, simple legs. From the bed she went to the dressing table. She discovered its skirt was fastened with small tacks. Quickly she ran down to the kitchen to fetch the hammer. Prying the tacks loose was a slow, tedious job. Tory tried hard not to tear the material, but many of the tacks were in so tight that it was impossible to get at them without tearing the organdy a little. When she finally had the dressing table stripped she stood back to examine her work, and her heart sank. Unadorned, it was an ugly, graceless piece of furniture.

Tory sat down on the chair to try to compose herself. By this time the room was a mess, with the bed torn apart and the dressing table naked. The whole room needs doing over, she thought to herself, morosely. A picture of the room she would like to have formed in her mind: a trim studio bed with a fitted cover on it and tons of tailored pillows, a blond, highly polished modern desk instead of the dressing table, a couple of sling-back bright red canvas chairs, and some striped Indian madras drapes. All contemporary and sleek, and no bow or ruffle or pink anyplace in the room. Tory could squint her eyes and almost see everything in the childish room that she suddenly despised disappear, and a glamorous, sophisticated, modern room take its place.

There probably wasn't a chance in the world that she could ever get such a room, but Tory decided then and there it was worth fighting for. At least it would give her something to think about. She started planning her campaign immediately.

That night at the supper table, after her mother had told her father, Ethan, and herself all about her busy day, and how lovely the library looked for Mrs. Honeycomb's party that evening, Tory casually introduced the subject of her room. "I was thinking I'd like to get a few things for my room," she said. "I have some of my birthday money left. I'd like to change my room around."

"Isn't that funny! Just the other day I saw some marvelous new chintzes at Hollander's. There was one I liked especially. I could run up some new curtains for you in no time." Mrs. Darling's eyes sparkled. "It would fit in perfectly with your bedspread and your chair; we'd have to make a new drape for your dressing table. . . ."

Tory squirmed uncomfortably. "Thanks very much, Mother, but I don't think I want chintz. As a matter of fact, I want to do the room entirely differently. Would I be able to buy a new bed?"

"A new bed?" Mrs. Darling's voice was shocked. "Tory, your bed is a reproduction of an heirloom."

"Mother, there's no such thing as a reproduction of an heirloom! Either something's an heirloom or it isn't."

Mr. Darling and Ethan had been silent during the conversation. Mr. Darling had long since adopted the policy of not interfering with his wife's activities, in which he included, for the most part, the managing of their two children. He was a quiet, amiable man, very busy with his job as an executive in a local electronics plant. He and Mrs. Darling very rarely had disagreements, and he viewed her doings with an air of amused tolerance. "As long as she doesn't insist I go to all those meetings with her, what she does is all right with me," he often said.

Now he interrupted and pointed out to his wife gently, "I think you mean an antique, dear."

"Well, it's more than just an antique," Mrs. Darling said indignantly. "It's a copy of a bed that's in a museum!"

"I don't care if Washington slept in it," Tory said hotly, "I'm sick of it. If I can't buy a new one, can I at least saw off the bedposts?" Tory eyed her mother steadily.

"Saw off the bedposts!" Her mother shrieked in horror. "Tory, you can't mean that. I can't imagine your even thinking such a thing!" Mrs. Darling was incredulous.

"You'd make a mess of it," Mr. Darling commented. "It would take a cabinetmaker to do a good job."

"Now Tory, darling," her mother spoke soothingly. "I'll be glad to do over a few things in your room. It's about due for a little redecorating. Perhaps you and Ethan can paint it over some week end. You just leave it to me, honey."

Tory gathered up her courage. "But I don't want to leave it to you," she said, her heart beating nervously. "I want to do it myself, in my own way." She leaned forward across the table. "Couldn't you give me whatever money you'd spend on my room and let me do it myself?" Her eyes went eagerly from her mother's face to her father's.

"I leave these things to your mother," Mr. Darling said diplomatically. "It's up to her."

"It's Tory's room! Why can't she have it the way she wants it?" Ethan demanded.

"Of course, I want her to be happy in her room," Mrs. Darling said. "This is the first time she's mentioned that she doesn't like it. But there are some things she is too young to know about. Imagine wanting to cut up a four-poster bed! And after all, I do know a little bit about it. Everyone in town comes to ask my advice about decorating. It would seem silly not to help and advise my own daughter."

"But, Mother, I—" Tory stopped short. She didn't want to hurt her mother's feelings. How could she say I don't like your taste, I don't want your advice, I want to do it on my own, my very own way?

"She wants to do it herself, Mom," Ethan said, putting his finger on the heart of the matter. "Why can't she?"

All eyes turned to Mrs. Darling. "I'm not saying she can't," she said, smiling placatingly, "but it doesn't really have to be a dinner-table discussion. Tory and I will discuss it later, and we'll work it out fine, I'm sure."

Tory's heart sank. She felt trapped. This is the end of my room, she thought desperately. She didn't know how to cope with her mother. She didn't know how to cope with all the contradictory emotions she felt: not wanting to hurt her mother's feelings; needing to fight off this recurring sense of being suffocated; loving her mother and hating her all at once; wishing she had the nerve to establish to her parents, in some dramatic and exciting way, that she was a person to reckon with. In a storybook she would flare up, stamp her foot, and make a scene—she would have them all cowering before her —but people didn't do that any more. How can you throw a temper tantrum when your parents are intelligent and kind, and you know they love you?

"By the way, Tory," her mother was saying in one of her sweet voices, "I met Mrs. Hopkins at the supermarket today. Poor thing, she's having a terrible time. Her husband's in the hospital with a heart attack, you know. She was buying dinner for Adam to eat alone, because she goes to the hospital every evening. So I told her to send Adam over here for his dinners while Mr. Hopkins stays in the hospital."

Tory stared at her mother in disbelief. "You asked Adam Hopkins over here for dinner every night? Why, Mother, I . . . I . . ." Tory didn't know what to say.

"But, Tory, I thought you'd be delighted. He's such an attractive boy, and you did go out with him. Besides,

I thought it was the neighborly thing to do." Mrs. Darling looked around the table pleasantly.

"Mother, why do *you* always have to do everything?" Tory wailed. "This town has a population of over five thousand, but you have to run the hospital, run the library, you have to invite Adam Hopkins over here every single night!"

"Your mother does a great many wonderful things," Mr. Darling said crisply.

"Why didn't she just ask him for one night?" Tory demanded.

"It didn't occur to me, and besides that wouldn't be much help to Mrs. Hopkins. This way she doesn't have to worry about him. She knows where he is, and she knows he's being fed. I don't think there's much money there, and with all their doctor bills, I'd like to do something."

"Well, you did it," Tory said furiously. There was no use trying to explain to her mother how awful it would be to have Adam come to dinner every night. It was the worst possible timing for Tory, just now when things were beginning to click between herself and Adam. This would spoil everything. He would think she was running after him, and if he did ask her for a date, it would be because he had to, to reciprocate for her mother's idiotic hospitality!

Her mother couldn't know all this, but why did she

have to stick her nose into everything! Why did she have to run everyone and everything, and spoil Tory's life?

Tory left the table immediately after supper and went upstairs to her room. She hadn't bothered to put her bed back together again, and the room was a shambles. But she was determined now, more than ever, not to let her mother win on this score. Even if the cold war turns into a hot one, she thought, I'm going to fight it out and do my room over my own way.

But when she thought of her mother and Adam she was discouraged. How can you fight someone who is good and charitable, and makes you feel small and selfish and unreasonable? Tory sat on top of her bed weary with it all. Here she was with the sweetest, kindest mother in the world, everyone in town said that, and yet she couldn't bear it, because she was being suffocated. It was all very perplexing.

That night Tory did something she had not done since she was a baby. She got undressed and went to bed while it was still light out; it wasn't even eight o'clock. She didn't go downstairs to say good night to anyone, but crawled into bed and cried herself to sleep.

Chapter 2

TORY awoke to the ringing of the telephone. It would be for her mother, she thought sleepily, and she'd probably sit at the phone for hours, rehashing last night's party for Mrs. Honeycomb. All the fuss about teenagers using the phone! If Tory ever talked that much, her mother would be furious. Unfair! Tory buried her head under the covers, and felt sheepish when her mother called and said that Amy was on the phone.

Barefoot, Tory went across the hall to her parents' bedroom, where her mother was holding the phone. Amy wanted to know what she was doing today, and Tory told her she'd call back later. The first thing she wanted to do was to settle her room with her mother. She could hear Ethan playing outside with his friends, and she decided this was as good a time as any.

"Mom, what about my room? Can I fix it over the way I want?" Tory asked.

Her mother was dressed and sitting at her small desk. The bed was already made and the room swept. "This is no time to discuss it, before you've even had breakfast. When you've eaten and done your room, and if there's time before I have to go out, we can sit down and talk about it. I have to do some telephoning now." Her mother smiled at her pleasantly.

"You're always so busy! What are you up to now?" Tory asked impatiently.

"Well, the Community Center wants to give some summer courses for adults, and they've asked me to help plan them. I'd love to get that marvelous man I had when I took that course at Yale on child psychology, if only he'd come up here. . . ."

"What did you learn about child psychology?"

"I think I learned a lot." Her mother laughed gaily. "You don't expect me to sit here and tell you in five minutes what I spent a whole winter studying, do you? Now run along, and we'll see if there's time to discuss your room."

I almost have to make an appointment to talk to my own mother, Tory thought resentfully, as she went back to her room. She put on her shorts and a shirt, went downstairs, and heaped a bowl with cold cereal and milk. She gulped down the food, washed out the bowl, and went back upstairs to get her bed made quickly. Twenty minutes had elapsed when she faced her mother again. Mrs. Darling was talking on the phone, and Tory waited patiently until she was finished. "Now can we talk?" she demanded, as soon as her mother had hung up the receiver.

"You certainly are in a hurry. What's your rush? Your room won't run away," Mrs. Darling said with a smile.

"I'd like to get things settled. What's your objection to my doing my room over?" Tory asked. She sat down on the edge of her mother's bed, trying not to wrinkle her mother's dainty white spread.

"I didn't say I objected." Mrs. Darling swung her chair around from her desk so that she could face Tory. She looked very businesslike, dressed in her striped shirtwaist dress and brown-and-white pumps, with her hair neatly brushed back from her forehead. "I'll be glad to help you do it. I've been thinking about it, and I have some ideas I think you'd like. For instance—"

"But Mother," Tory interrupted. "I don't want you to help me. I want to do it myself. Why can't I?"

"Tory, when you talk about cutting down a four-poster bed, the truth is I don't think you're old enough to do a room by yourself. Furniture is expensive, and we can't throw money away."

"But it *is* my bed, isn't it?"

"Well, yes and no." Mrs. Darling picked up a pad

from her desk and started doodling. "It is your bed, but you can't chop it up," she said softly.

"If it's mine, why can't I do what I want with it?" Tory asked. "I remember distinctly when you did my room over. It was for my tenth birthday, and the whole room was a birthday present for me. So everything in it is mine, isn't it? You can't very well take back a birthday present, can you?" Tory looked directly into her mother's blue eyes.

"Darling, I wouldn't dream of it. Yes, that furniture is yours. But I still can't allow you to take a perfectly fine bed and ruin it. I would be very irresponsible if I let you do that." Her mother returned Tory's look evenly, but her mouth was pursed unhappily.

"But Mother, a bed's only a piece of furniture. It isn't as if I were going around being a juvenile delinquent or something. It's my bed, and if I want to cut it up, that's my business. I'm not destroying someone else's property. Besides, I happen to think I won't be destroying it, that it will look better."

"That's ridiculous! You'll ruin that bed! You're too young to know or understand. That's why I can't let you do certain things by yourself yet. I really don't have time to sit here all morning discussing anything this absurd. The answer is no, and that's all there is to it." Mrs. Darling put the pad in her hand back on the desk with an air of finality.

"You don't get the point, Mother! I haven't even

decided what I want to do with the bed. But I want the right to do it. My taste and your taste may be very different. You've taken all those courses in child psychology. I thought you were supposed to let me make my own mistakes. You're as bad as the worst Victorian mother!" Tory's face was flushed, and she knew she was talking much too loudly.

"Why, Tory!" Mrs. Darling's voice was shocked. She blinked her eyes as if she might be going to cry. "You make me feel very bad. I only try to do what is right for you and Ethan."

Tory felt like a monster. She knelt down on the floor beside her mother and put her arms around her mother's slim waist. "I'm sorry. I didn't mean to hurt your feelings. It's just that . . ." she broke off lamely. She felt unsettled, as she did so often with her mother, because everything was left hanging in mid-air.

"Mother, if I don't have a pretty room, I'll be the one to suffer, not you. Please let me try," Tory persisted.

"I don't suppose I can stop you," her mother answered. "Why don't you give me a plan of what you want to do, and then we can discuss it again?" Mrs. Darling smiled brightly at her daughter, pleased with her solution of the problem.

"But that's not the same." Tory felt as if she were drowning and someone had thrown her a life belt full of holes. "I thought you would give me whatever money you and Daddy decided I could spend on my room, and then I could do it myself, probably over the summer." That last was a mistake; Tory realized it as soon as she said it.

"The summer's still quite a way off," Mrs. Darling said, patting Tory's head. "That gives us plenty of time to think about it. I'm sure we can work it out so that we'll both be happy. And, in the meantime, your room isn't that bad, is it?" She smiled at Tory affectionately. "You loved it so when you got it, remember? I'll never forget your face when we marched you in there on your birthday."

"That was a long time ago, Mom." Tory got up and walked slowly back to her room. She felt exhausted and unhappy. Talk, talk, talk! Nothing had been decided, and she was convinced that nothing would be. She'd go on living with this room until she got married probably. Her mother might change the curtains or the bedspread, but the room would still be the same. Her mother always won. She never actually said no, but she didn't say yes either.

Tory wandered around the room restlessly. She felt as if she were going to explode with unused energy. She thought vaguely that redecorating her room would help her to discover her real self, help her to learn what kind of person she really was. Even her mother was fond of saying you can tell what a woman is like the minute you walk into her house and see her furnishings. Now her hopes were dashed, and she felt restless and disconsolate. She phoned Amy back, and Amy asked her to come over. Tory agreed, hoping that she would cheer her up.

Amy's father was dead and her mother worked. There were four younger children in the family, and Amy spent a lot of time taking care of them and had a great many responsibilities at home. She was a small, slightly built, energetic girl, with a serious, gentle face and a bright smile. She greeted Tory from the kitchen, where she was washing a stack of dishes.

"Where are the kids?" Tory asked. "It's so quiet around here."

"The boys are outside playing, and I had to send Stacey up to her room. She's being terrible this morning."

Tory took a towel and started drying the rinsed dishes. She looked at her friend admiringly. "I don't know how you do it," she said. "You really run this house. I think it's wonderful that your mother lets you."

"She doesn't have much choice," Amy said with a laugh. "We can't afford a maid, so I'm it. It's a pain in the neck, if you ask me. I don't see anything so wonderful about it."

"At least your mother doesn't treat you like a baby. I don't know. . . ." She was thinking that Mrs. Pitcher was a working woman, and didn't have time to go to all the meetings and read all the books that her own mother did. Yet she seemed to have better sense about how to treat her daughter. Tory didn't say all that to Amy. "Sometimes I wish my mother worked," she said, "then she wouldn't have time to watch over everything so much. Not that she's home a lot, she isn't, but she fusses about everything." She told Amy about her room, ending up forlornly, "I suppose I'll have to go on living with her little doodads and chintzes forever, as if I were a two-year-old. I'd love to throw everything out and have a contemporary room."

"Maybe she'll let you. She didn't absolutely say no, did she?" Amy asked hopefully.

Tory shook her head. "She never absolutely says no. She loves to discuss things. She likes to pretend she's treating me as if I were very grown up, but she always has her own way. Do you ever hate your mother?" she asked Amy abruptly.

Amy looked at Tory with anxious eyes. "I don't think so, not really." She spoke slowly. "Sometimes I get awfully angry at her, but I don't think I ever hate her. You don't hate yours, either. I'm sure you don't," she added reassuringly.

Tory stared out the window, her face troubled. "I'm not sure. . . . I'm afraid I do, sometimes. It makes me feel awful. I know she's good and kind and sweet. She's a million times better than I'll ever be, all the things she does for people, and for the town. But sometimes I feel as if I just can't stand living in the same house with her any more. I feel so ashamed of myself when I'm away from her, and I'm sure I love her. Then bang, when I'm with her again, she does something that irritates me terribly, and it starts all over. I don't know what to do."

"What can you do?" Amy asked. "Besides, I don't believe you really hate her. You're just upset now about your room. You'll get over it."

"I hope so," Tory said. But instead of feeling hopeful, she felt dissatisfied and worried.

The two girls spent the day together. Tory helped Amy clean up the house, and then they took sun baths in back. When it got too hot out in the sun, they sat on Amy's back porch and talked.

Amy was going steady with Woodie Parker, and the two girls talked about him and other boys and girls in school. "It must be nice to have someone to count on, the way you have Woodie," Tory mused aloud.

Amy looked surprised. "I like it. But you always said you didn't want to go steady with anyone."

"I know," Tory said pensively, and she let out a deep sigh. "I guess I've never met anyone I liked that much, but it might be nice."

"What about Adam? Don't you like him?" Amy asked, with a teasing smile.

"I do like him," Tory said soberly, "I think I could like him a lot. Of course, I don't know him very well yet—" She sat up suddenly. "Oh, I didn't tell you what my mother did!" She looked at Amy woefully. "She's invited him for supper every night while his father's in the hospital. Isn't that awful?" U. S. 1190653

"It's really very nice of her. Why is it so awful? Now you'll see him every night," Amy said calmly.

"That's not the point. I'll see him, all right," she answered sarcastically. "It just spoils everything. Now he'll think I cooked this up and that I'm running after him. If he asks me out, it'll only be out of politeness. My mother always has to meddle with everything!" Tory ended up with exasperation.

"I see what you mean," Amy said thoughtfully. "I don't know what you can do about it, though. You're not going to change your mother. Everyone in town thinks she's wonderful."

"I know." Tory nodded her head dolefully. "She *is* wonderful. She's always doing things for people, she belongs to everything, but she's never home. I wish she was just an ordinary mother."

"You wouldn't like it if she were home all the time either," Amy said.

"If she didn't mix into my affairs, I would." Tory

pulled herself up from the chaise where she had been sitting. "I guess I'd better be going home now." She felt a nervous tremor of apprehension at the thought of Adam's coming to their house for supper. It would be awful having him at the dinner table, what with Ethan's rowdiness, and her mother reciting all the little events of the day. As if anyone cared about Mrs. Honeycomb and Mrs. This and Mrs. That, what they did, and what they wore! If they ever had interesting conversation at the dinner table it would be different.

Tory was about to leave when Amy's mother came home with a friend. She introduced the girls to Miss Northrup, and then turned to her and said, "Tory is Mrs. Darling's daughter. You worked with Mrs. Darling in the Cancer Campaign, didn't you?"

"Indeed, I did," Miss Northrup said enthusiastically. "She's a marvelous woman. Such energy and drive! You have a wonderful mother, dear," she said, smiling at Tory.

"Yes, I know," Tory said meekly. "It was nice meeting you." She shook hands and said good-by.

Tory walked home slowly. Mrs. Darling's daughter! How many times had she been introduced as Mrs. Darling's daughter! Wouldn't she ever be Tory Darling, someone in her own right? She sometimes felt that she was so many different persons she was no one at all. Being Mrs. Darling's daughter was only one part of her, the part of her that she liked the least. But as Amy's friend she was a completely separate person. The Tory Darling who went to school was someone still different, and she varied from class to class. In English, which she loved, she felt intelligent, and when Mrs. Holcomb praised one of her compositions, she wondered if one day she might become a serious writer. Then, in the very next class, which was chemistry, she felt like the biggest, clumsiest fool that ever was—she couldn't remember any of the formulas, somehow her burettes would always break, and no matter how carefully she started an experiment, it always ended up a terrible mess.

So who was she really?

Tory realized that it was getting late and she should be at home to help her mother set the table for supper, yet she felt reluctant to get there. When she finally turned into the driveway, she knew instantly that Adam was already there. She could hear her mother's light voice floating through the open windows and Adam's deep voice in contrast. She went through the house to the kitchen and found to her mortification that Adam was there helping her mother. He was whipping cream with her mother's electric beater.

Adam gave her a bright smile and said hello. Tory smiled back at him dumbly. His very proximity put her into a turmoil. He was a good head taller than she, very slim and dark, with a quiet quality about him. Tory never knew what he was thinking, which was one of his fascinating traits for her.

"How do you like my new cook?" her mother said gaily. "He's making dessert."

"I hope it doesn't turn into butter," Adam commented, peering into the bowl where the white swirls of heavy cream were thickening.

"Would you like me to do it, Mom," Tory asked self-consciously, "or should I set the table?"

"I wouldn't part with this for anything," Adam said with a smile.

"The table's all set," her mother said. "Adam beat you to it. He certainly is well-trained."

What's he supposed to do, say no to your ordering him around, Tory thought to herself. She bit her lip to keep from saying something unpleasant. "He's certainly working for his supper," she remarked.

"I like it," Adam said simply.

He did seem to be enjoying himself. Here's another one, Tory thought morosely, who'll be telling me what a wonderful mother I have. There must be something wrong with me, she told herself sternly, feeling as if she were the only one out of step.

"Tory, hadn't you better go upstairs and take a shower before dinner," Mrs. Darling called to her from the dining room. "You look hot and untidy."

Tory felt herself blush furiously. "Thanks a lot," she murmured, and ran out of the kitchen and up the stairs without daring to look at Adam.

That was exactly the kind of thing she had been afraid of when her mother said Adam would be around every evening. How can you be glamorous and interesting to a boy when he sees you this way at home, with your own mother saying that you look hot and messy! This was togetherness with a vengeance.

Tory tried to smooth her angry face as she looked at herself in the mirror. Her mother said if she got angry too often she'd get wrinkles. Well, she'd sure enough get wrinkles if life went on like this. Why, oh why, didn't she have a nice, quiet mother who stayed at home and did something sensible like knitting or gardening! She stared balefully at the four-poster bed. If there were a saw handy, she'd take those bedposts off this minute, no questions asked.

By the time she had finished with her shower and was dressed, her father and Ethan were home, and it was time to sit down to supper. Adam was at the table already, seeming as much at home as a member of the family, teasing Ethan, helping her mother to pass the plates. Tory felt like the guest, the outsider, as Adam dished some potatoes onto her plate. "Thank you," she murmured.

"You're welcome," Adam said solemnly, but he gave

her a sympathetic look that made her suddenly wonder if he realized how uncomfortable she felt. This gave her small comfort. To think of going through this every night! What on earth could be more deadly for any romance that might develop between them!

Chapter 3

Spring vacation had come and gone and now it was almost the end of May. Through the open window Tory watched a phoebe flying back and forth to the nest she was building. Industriously, the bird placed each small twig in place against the porch light, a perennial favorite nesting place. Each year her nest was the source of a minor family quarrel. Mr. Darling insisted that they prevent her from making it in that spot, warning that she and her babies would create a mess all over the porch floor, as they invariably did. Tory and Ethan flatly refused to touch the nest, while Mrs. Darling begged everyone to do something, but she never suggested what.

Tory observed the bird and listened to the conversation taking place in her living room with very much the same reaction: she had been through it all before.

She and Amy had been asked by Mrs. Darling to attend a P.T.A. committee meeting that was working on the final school dance of the year. Mrs. Darling, president of the P.T.A., was acting as chairman of the committee and of the meeting. The two girls were sitting on the floor in the crowded room; Tory's mind kept wandering, because she knew in advance what practically everyone present would have to say.

Mrs. Schultz, who wore flowered print dresses and hats adorned with artificial roses, interrupted every few minutes to tell how they did things in Oak Park, a fashionable suburb of Chicago, where she used to live. Right now she was announcing that, "we always asked the boys in the freshman class to park the cars. It gave them something to do and made them feel important." She looked smugly around the room for approval, as if she had made an invaluable contribution.

No one paid much attention, because three other ladies were all talking at once. Mrs. Harris, in a crisp shirtmaker dress, was reading her notes aloud, apparently to herself. With a toothy smile, Mrs. Dunbar was describing her last bridge game to a pretty young woman sitting next to her, while Mrs. Darling tried politely, but firmly, to call the meeting to order.

Tory's and Amy's eyes met. "I don't know why they want us here," Tory whispered. "They're only going to talk all afternoon anyway."

"Sh-sh," Amy admonished.

Mrs. Darling had finally got some order, and was setting up committees to take care of all the necessary arrangements. One committee for refreshments, one for decorations, one for publicity, one for getting the band, and one for printing the tickets. Tory couldn't help admiring her mother's efficiency. She seemed to know exactly the right thing to say to each person there. She flattered Mrs. Schultz and she humored Mrs. Dunbar; she made the most of Mrs. Harris's notes. In no time at all everything was set up and in order, and even Amy whispered to Tory how well Mrs. Darling had handled everyone.

"Yes, I know," Tory said. "She's terrific." She didn't mean to sound grudging, and yet she couldn't help but wonder about her mother's sweetness and charm to everyone there. Tory happened to know that Mrs. Darling had no use for Mrs. Schultz. As a matter of fact, she had heard her mother say that she considered Mrs. Schultz a pretentious snob. Wasn't she being hypocritical? Tory mused.

Mrs. Darling was serving tea when the phone rang. Tory answered it, and an unfamiliar man's voice asked for her mother. "Probably someone trying to sell me a freezer," Mrs. Darling remarked, excusing herself from her guests.

When Mrs. Darling came back from the phone, however, she looked flustered. "Who was it?" Tory asked.

Her mother blushed furiously. "It's the most extraor-
dinary thing—I don't know how to tell you—" She
addressed the roomful of women as well as Tory. "It
was Mr. Carmichael, from the Chamber of Commerce.
They've decided this year to give an award to the best
mother—just from Huntington County. They want to
interest women in the Chamber of Commerce. It's all a
big promotion scheme of course. . . ."

"But what's it got to do with you?" Tory asked.

Mrs. Darling laughed uncertainly. "Mr. Carmichael
called to say that they had picked me. Can you imagine?
Me, the Mother of the Year!"

Mrs. Darling was interrupted by a babble of voices.
Everyone wanted to be the first to kiss her and to congratulate her.

"It's wonderful . . . how marvelous . . . our own Doro-
thea Darling. . . ." There was one exclamation after
another.

"And what do you think, Tory?" Her mother turned
to her. "I'm really not that good a mother to you and
Ethan, but I do try hard. . . ."

"I think it's wonderful," Tory said, and she too
kissed her mother on the cheek. Her feelings were
mixed, and she hoped her face didn't betray the emotions she felt, one chasing after another. Of course, she
was proud of her mother, but mixed with the pride was

a sense of both apprehension and resentment. She was glad that her mother had been chosen for such an honor, but heavens, Tory thought to herself, what is she going to be like now! She wondered what the Chamber of Commerce really knew about her mother, aside from seeing her name on a lot of committees. What did they know about how she was at home when she was with her family?

Finally all the ladies left, and although Tory begged her to stay, Amy had to go, too. She was the last to leave, however, and Mrs. Darling turned to the two girls aghast. "Oh my," she said, "we all got so excited about that silly phone call, we never put you two on any committee. I think you should act unofficially on all of them. You can work with the publicity committee, after all you're in the best position to see that the tickets get pushed at school. And we would love your advice on the refreshments and decorations. You will do it, won't you?"

"You mean we'll do all the work!" Tory stated candidly.

Her mother laughed. "Not really, just part of it. You don't mind, do you?"

"No, of course not," Amy put in quickly. "We'll be glad to help." She gave Tory a warning look that said, take it easy, you and I will work it out together later, so don't worry.

Tory took the hint and she kept quiet. But after Amy left, Mrs. Darling turned to her again, and asked once more, as if she wanted reassurance, what Tory thought about the choice of her as Mother of the Year of Huntington County.

"I think it's fine," Tory said frankly. "But I don't understand how you can be so sweet and lovely with that awful Mrs. Schultz. You yourself say she's an awful snob."

"Yes, I know," Mrs. Darling spoke defensively. "But I have to work with her. I didn't put her on the committee, she volunteered. I can't be rude to her. And she will be helpful."

"Well, it seems very hypocritical to me," Tory said.

Mrs. Darling sighed. "It's difficult to explain. You are so terribly honest, Tory dear, and I admire you for it. But it's not always the way one gets along with people. Sometimes one must hide one's personal feelings. It's rather complicated, and, I suppose, one of the sad things about growing up. One cannot always be simple and direct and honest."

"Then I don't think very much of grownups, if they can't be direct and honest. I intend to be," Tory said.

"Then I'm afraid you will hurt people and they won't like you," Mrs. Darling told her.

"If I have to lie to people to make them like me, I just won't bother," Tory said.

"It's not a question of lying," her mother said indignantly. "I don't lie to people, either! It's a matter of being diplomatic and not hurting people's feelings."

"I'm sorry. I still think it's two-faced," Tory said stubbornly.

Her feelings about her mother had not changed since spring vacation. If anything, since Adam had been coming to dinner every night, they had gotten worse. Adam, too, seemed to have come under the spell of her mother's charm. Unfortunately, his father was going to have to stay in the hospital for several months, and Mrs. Darling had insisted that he continue to take his dinners with them. Tory had no choice but to accept having him around, but she was still resentful of the arrangement. As she moaned to Amy, "It's spoiled everything. I don't want to be just friends with Adam. I want something entirely different. So he asks me to go to the movies with him once in a while—what else can he do? He has to be polite. There's certainly nothing exciting between us."

That night at the supper table Mrs. Darling was gayer and more talkative than ever. She was keyed up by the honor from the Chamber of Commerce, and after the family, including Adam, had commented on how exciting it was, Mrs. Darling went on to speak about the plans for the forthcoming dance.

"We want this to be the best dance the school ever had," Mrs. Darling concluded.

"Why?" Tory asked.

Mrs. Darling laughed. "Why not?"

"When your mother does a job, she likes to do it well," Mr. Darling said. "Naturally she wants this to be the best dance."

"My teacher says we shouldn't care so much about being the best in the class," Ethan remarked.

"That's a funny thing for a teacher to say," Mrs. Darling said. "Why shouldn't you want to be best?"

"She says we care too much about marks and winning games. She says it's what we do that counts, and how. She says we're too competitive."

"She's right," Tory said. "She must be a very good teacher."

"I'm not so sure," her mother said. "This whole country thrives on free competition. That's one of the things that makes us so great."

"Well, that's true," Mr. Darling said thoughtfully. "But in economics it's different. Free enterprise is one thing. But I'm not so sure everybody should feel he has to win. Someone has to lose, too, and being a good loser is important."

Adam, who had been listening quietly, looked at Tory and came to her defense. "I agree with Tory. I think we put too much emphasis on winning and getting to the top. I think that's why my father's in the hospital. He's a machinist, and he always felt he had to produce the most, more than anyone else. He was always pushing himself to be the best—and now look where he is. Flat on his back, and he can't work at all."

"That's what I mean," Tory said, looking at Adam gratefully.

"Heavens, how did we get off on this!" Mrs. Darling changed the subject lightly. "We were talking about the dance. I want you two to work hard on selling tickets," she said to Adam and Tory. "I hope every girl in town gets asked to this dance. I think I'll buy you a new dress," she added to Tory, and then glanced at her husband. "I saw a lovely pale pink chiffon downtown the other day, it was simple and beautiful. You'll be the belle of the ball in it."

"Does she really need a new dress?" Mr. Darling asked.

"Oh, Mother! I'll have to be *asked* to the dance first."

"You'll be asked, I'm not worried about that!" Mrs. Darling looked from Tory to Adam smilingly. Then she answered her husband. "Her old dress looks shabby. It's time for a new one."

Tory felt her face flush, and at that moment she could have murdered her mother cheerfully. Adam grinned at her, and Tory had a terrible feeling that maybe he was laughing at her. This is the end, she thought to herself. The very end. Now I'll never, never be able to go with him. Tory could hardly wait until supper was over, when she could excuse herself and leave the table.

But Adam was faster than she was. He stopped her before she got to the door, and said, "If you're not doing anything tonight, would you feel like going for a walk? Or we could go to a movie if you like?" He was looking down at her, but after one swift glance into his eyes, she didn't trust herself to look up at him. She wasn't quite sure what was behind the quizzical expression on his face: was it sympathy, humor, or something more? His sympathy would be more than she could bear.

"Perhaps we could go for a short walk after I finish with the dishes," she said.

"Let me help you," Adam suggested.

"Hey, Adam," Ethan was calling from the yard. "You promised to play ball with me, remember?"

"I forgot—I did promise Ethan. I'll be outside, whenever you're ready."

Adam turned and went out. Tory avoided her mother's eyes when she joined her in the kitchen. She was much too angry to say anything.

"What a lovely boy," Mrs. Darling said, staring out the window, dreamily. "Isn't he sweet to play with Ethan?"

"What choice does he have?" Tory asked. "I bet he hates coming over here every night, having to play ball with Ethan and be nice to me, and running errands for you. If I were he I'd rather stay home and eat alone!"

"It's possible that he enjoys being nice. Some people do, dear." Tory glanced at her mother to see if she was being sarcastic, but Mrs. Darling's blue eyes were serenely innocent.

Tory sighed. There was no use discussing Adam with her mother. Mrs. Darling would never understand the complications of all the remarks she made in front of him, and how impossible she was making it for Tory to date him at all.

How could a mother be so smart about some things and so dumb about others? Tory wondered whether her mother ever suspected how many millions of miles apart the two of them really were. She had heard her mother say, "Tory can't keep a secret; that girl tells me everything!" Yet there was a whole part of Tory's life that her mother knew nothing about. What of all the private thoughts she shared with no one, not even with Amy, and certainly never with her mother? The little daydreams about Adam, or some unknown boy she made up, and the exciting things they might be do-ing . . . or the faraway places where they might be going . . . or even the thoughts Tory had about her mother herself!

By the time Tory had finished the dishes, Adam was waiting for her. "Which way do you want to go?" he asked, as they stepped outside. It was still light out, and the sky was tinted with the delicate yellows and pinks of summer's twilight, giving the familiar, prosaic street the coloring of an old Dutch painting.

"Let's go down to the river," Tory suggested.

They walked mostly in silence until they left the sidewalk and turned into an overgrown dirt road, no longer used by automobiles. This seemed to be a signal for Adam to speak what was on his mind. He cleared his throat and plunged in. "What's the matter, Tory?" he asked. "You've been acting awfully funny ever since your mother invited me to come eat with you. Don't you like having me around?"

Tory met his eyes, and then she looked away. "I don't mind having you around," she mumbled. "I haven't been acting funny. You just imagine it," she said more distinctly. She couldn't tell him that she actually didn't want him around every night, because he would never understand her reasons. Besides, you can't tell a boy that you feel romantic about him and that you wish he would feel romantic about you.

"Well, maybe I am imagining it," Adam said, looking unconvinced. "I feel so indebted to your mother," he continued earnestly. "I hope she knows how much we appreciate what she's doing. It's such a help to my mother. She keeps saying all the time what a relief it is to know I'm taken care of every night. She says she doesn't know how she'll ever thank your mother."

"Tell her not to worry about that. My mother loves having you—we all do," Tory said hurriedly. "And it's no bother, honestly. Feeding four people or five, what's the difference?"

"Well, it's great." Adam lapsed back into silence. They sat down on a large, flat rock at the river's edge and watched the gulls fly down, looking for their evening meal.

Finally Adam broke the silence. "I'd like you to come to the dance with me," he said. He was throwing pebbles into the water, and Tory watched him carefully select a thin, flat round pebble and skim it over the water expertly. He didn't look up at her, and Tory felt a diffidence in him. He's only asking me to be polite, she thought to herself bitterly, and because my mother as much as suggested it!

"Thanks very much," Tory said, "but I don't think I'm going to the dance." The words came out unexpectedly; they were not what she had intended to say, and yet, once she had spoken, she was convinced that that was what she wanted to do. She didn't want to have anything whatsoever to do with the dance her mother was so busily organizing.

"Why not?" Adam didn't seem particularly surprised; it was almost as if that was the answer he had expected.

"I don't think it's going to be any good. All the kids are coming, even the eighth-graders, and a million parents will be there. It's going to be awful."

"You'd better not let your mother hear you say that," Adam said with a grin. "She thinks it's going to be great."

"Well, please don't quote me," Tory said. She wondered for a minute if she could trust him. Would he go back and tell her mother she was blackballing the dance? She guiltily pushed the thought from her mind and felt ashamed that such a thought had even occurred to her. Yet she didn't know what he was thinking about, and he seemed to feel as strained with her as she did with him. Here they were, all alone, and they could hardly talk to each other. Tory wished she knew how to get them back to where they had been before her mother took over.

Adam turned around suddenly and his arm brushed hers. He gave her a swift look, and turned away. For the first time in her life, Tory longed for a boy to take her in his arms and kiss her. The abruptness of the thought shocked her. She had never felt this way before! It seemed strange to be sitting here in the mild evening twilight wanting so much to be kissed, wondering, if she wished hard enough, whether Adam would respond. She didn't believe in mental telepathy, and yet there had been something in his eyes as he turned away from her that made her wonder. . . .

"I guess we'd better be going," Adam said, standing up. "I told your mother I'd take some lists for the dance over to Mrs. Harris's, and my mother will be coming home from the hospital soon."

"How is your father? Is he getting any better?" Tory asked. She never knew whether to ask after him or not. Usually Adam's face clouded over whenever anyone spoke about his father, and she thought that perhaps he'd rather not answer questions.

"I don't think so," Adam spoke slowly. "I have a feeling he's never going to leave the hospital—not alive anyway."

"Oh, Adam, you don't know. The doctors haven't said that, have they?"

Adam shook his head. "Not outright, no. But I know my father. I can tell by the way he looks and acts. He's lost interest in living."

"He probably just seems that way, because he has to be quiet. I'm sure he'll get well," Tory said gently.

"I hope so." They walked back side by side, careful not to touch each other. It was an odd walk, Tory thought, and she wondered why Adam had suggested it. If he'd had something special he wanted to talk about, he must have decided not to follow it up.

For the next couple of weeks all Tory heard at home was talk about the dance. Each night she tried to get up enough courage to tell her mother that she wasn't going, but so far she had been unable to do it. Finally her mother insisted that she go downtown with her to shop for a dress the next afternoon, and Tory knew the time had come.

She waited until after supper, when she and her mother were alone in the kitchen doing the dishes. "I'll pick you up at school tomorrow," Mrs. Darling said, "and we can shop."

"I don't need a new dress," Tory started to object.

"Well, I think you should have one. You don't mind, do you?" Mrs. Darling laughed at the idea. "I never heard of a girl not wanting a new evening gown."

"You don't understand, Mother. I don't need a new dress. I'm not going to the dance."

Mrs. Darling nearly dropped the plate in her hand. She stared at Tory unbelievingly. "You're not going? I. . . . I never heard of such a thing. It's ridiculous. Adam asked you, didn't he?" Mrs. Darling's face was incredulous.

"Did you tell him to ask me?" Tory asked sharply.

"Of course not. Why should I? I knew he was going to ask you. Don't tell me he didn't, I can't believe it."

Tory felt near tears of anger. "Yes, he asked me. That's exactly *why* I'm not going. Do you think I want to go with someone who *has* to ask me? Adam's the last person in the world I'd go with. I wish you wouldn't interfere with everything. I wish you would stay at home the way other mothers do. President of the P.T.A., Mother of the Year.... It makes me sick!" Tory had said more than she meant to, but once she started she couldn't stop. And I'm not sorry either, she thought to herself. By now she couldn't keep the tears back, and she flew out of the kitchen and up the stairs to her room.

As the tears rolled down her face, she thought, I mean every word of it, but what's the use now? She heard her mother's footsteps coming up the stairs, and her mother's rap on the door. Mrs. Darling barely waited for Tory's response to come in, before she entered the room. Her eyes were filled with tears, and she looked as if she would burst into sobs herself any minute.

"Tory dear, you're crying." Mrs. Darling's voice was quavering. "I feel awful. I'll resign from everything.... I had no idea you felt that way about the things I do. I just like to keep busy, and to do my share, but if it upsets you so, I'll give it all up. I can resign from the P.T.A. I can't very well tell the Chamber of Commerce to unelect me, but that won't take up any time. I'll stay home and we'll do things together—oh, my poor baby, have I been neglecting you?" She put her arms around Tory and held her close.

Tory squirmed uncomfortably. "Oh, Mother, it's not

that, forget it. I don't want you to resign or anything like that. I—I wasn't thinking, I'm sorry."

"But darling, you look so unhappy. I really do want to be a good mother. You and Ethan mean more to me than anything in the world—there's nothing I wouldn't do if it made you happy."

"I know, Mom. I'm sorry. Just forget it, please."

"But what about the dance? I wouldn't feel right if you stayed home. Here I am chairman of it, and I have the prettiest daughter in town—and not to have her at the dance! What will people think!"

"I really don't care what people think, Mom, but I'm not going to that dance. Tell them I'm sick, I don't care. Say anything you want."

"But why won't you come? You do like Adam, don't you? I can tell. . . . I can see the way he looks at you and the way you pretend he's not there. Did you two have a spat?" Mrs. Darling had dried her tears, and now she had a teasing smile on her face.

"No, we didn't have a spat." Tory repeated her mother's words distastefully. "I mean fight," she added. "Spat! Where did you dig up that word, from some Victorian novel?"

"Spat is a perfectly good English word," Mrs. Darling said defensively. "But Tory," she continued in a coaxing tone, "please tell me why you don't want to go to the dance. You and I have always been good friends, and it would be very painful for me not to have you there. You don't want to hurt me, do you?"

All she thinks about is herself, Tory thought resentfully. *She* would be hurt, *she* wouldn't feel right, what would people think of *her*. "Of course, I don't want to hurt you," Tory said indignantly. "I have my own private reasons for not wanting to go, and I'd rather not discuss them." By this time Tory wasn't sure she could ever put into words why this dance had become abominable to her. It was partly because of the reasons she had given Adam; it had been dubbed a "kids' dance" by most of her friends in school, even though they were going to it. But her main reason, she suspected, was her mother's connection with the dance. She simply didn't want to play the role of "Mrs. Darling's daughter" with her mother's friends watching every move she made.

Tory dreaded the night of the dance. Adam didn't come for supper that evening. Ever since their strange walk down to the river, there was a definite barrier between them that upset Tory, but she didn't know how to break through it. Adam was taking Liz Brooks, a very pretty girl in Tory's class, to the dance, and Tory felt that she had completely lost him.

Friday, the day of the dance, the phone kept ringing for her mother; people were calling to check on last minute details. At five o'clock Mrs. Darling was in the kitchen having a cup of tea and giving instructions to Tory on what to give Ethan, her father, and herself for dinner. Mr. Darling hated dances, especially with a bunch of teen-agers, as he put it, so he was going to a ball game with Ethan instead. "A much more sensible way to spend an evening," he stated.

"I have to get dressed and be there a little after six," Mrs. Darling said. "I have to be sure the punch gets made and the flowers are arranged, and someone must be there to greet the orchestra. . . ."

"You have all those committees, Mother," Tory reminded her. "I don't see why you have to do it all. You'd think you were running the dance all by yourself."

"Sometimes I think I am," Mrs. Darling admitted. "You don't know these women the way I do. Everything has to be checked on. Someone has to do it, and as president of the P.T.A. and chairman of the dance committee, it's my job."

"A good executive makes other people work," Tory said tartly.

"They did work," Mrs. Darling remonstrated. "But I still have to check. I wish you would change your mind and come with me. It would be a great help to me to have you there." Mrs. Darling looked at Tory pleadingly.

Tory shook her head emphatically. "No thanks. Not

me. I'll stay here and take care of your husband and son."

Tory breathed a sigh of relief when her mother finally left. Amy, too, had called once more to ask Tory if she didn't want to change her mind and go with her and Woodie, but Tory declined firmly.

After supper Mr. Darling and Ethan left for their ball game. They asked Tory to go with them, but she insisted that she would rather stay home. She wanted to be alone. She was up in her room when she saw Adam come out of his house and get into his father's car. He looked stunning in a white jacket and dark slacks. She had never seen Adam dressed up this way. He was carrying a small corsage in his hand. She watched him get into the car, put the corsage gently on the seat beside him, and adjust the seat for his long legs. His face had a scrubbed glow to it that made him especially appealing, like a little boy going to a party. Tory's heart turned over with tenderness for him, and then resentment for herself, at life, and at the whole world, because she wouldn't be the girl sitting beside him and wearing his flowers.

The fact that she was partly to blame didn't help. She could have said yes to his stilted invitation, if she had really wanted to, but what would have been the use? She would have been conscious every minute that it was merely a duty invitation. He must have been relieved when she said no, and he could take pretty Liz Brooks.

The car roared out of Adam's driveway and down the street. Tory's heart pounded with the noise of the engine. Then the block was quiet. The house was so still Tory could hear her heart beating. As she looked around her room, the girlish sweetness of it seemed more stifling than ever. "Well, that's one thing I can do something about," she said aloud.

Hastily she ran downstairs to the garage where her father kept his tools. She found a saw hanging on a nail; she grabbed it and ran back to her room. First she stood up on a chair and ripped the canopy from the top of her bed, letting it fall in a heap on the floor. Deliberately she viewed the pine bedposts. She selected a certain spot, just above a little curve, for sawing. When the post was cut, she could finish off the raw top, with a little sanding, and make it look like a knob. With quick, nervous strokes, she attacked the first bedpost. She sawed and sawed; it seemed to take forever before it was ready to topple over. When it finally fell onto the floor her heart sank. But it was too late now. Frantically she attacked the other three, one by one, until the bed was shorn of its tall, slender posts.

She ran down to the garage to put the saw back on its nail, and then came back upstairs more slowly to survey her work. She stuffed the canopy and the four sawed-off posts into the closet, feeling like a criminal trying to hide the evidence. The bed stared at her nakedly, and the four raw wooden ends seemed to be looking at her accusingly, almost as if they were human flesh and would start to bleed at any moment.

She felt like crying, but she assured herself stubbornly that she liked it much better. The room looks larger, she argued silently, and it will be wonderful not to have to sleep under that awful top any more. She flopped down on the bed, on her back, and it did seem nice to have the bed open and free. She felt as if she could breathe easily for the first time in months.

Tory closed the door and got undressed. It was very early, but she didn't want to see anyone or have any of the family come into her room. She wasn't ready to have them see what she had done. After reading awhile in bed, she fell asleep. She didn't hear Ethan or her father come home, but she did turn over, half-awake, when her mother arrived.

Tory heard a car, and suddenly she woke up completely. She was certain Adam had brought her mother home. Running to the window, she saw Adam saying good night to her mother, with Liz sitting in the car. Tory ran back to bed and put her head under the covers. She heard her mother tiptoe up the stairs and hesitate a few seconds at her door. Tory prayed fervently that she wouldn't come in and sighed with relief when she heard the door to her parents' room open and close gently.

But the rest of the night Tory slept restlessly. She turned and tossed and had terrible nightmares about wandering through a huge forest looking for a tree to chop down. Every time she found the right one and reached for the ax, the tree disappeared. Each time she woke up with a start and saw Adam and Liz close together, whispering. She couldn't put their faces out of her mind until she fell back into her restless sleep once more.

Chapter 4

THE next morning Tory awoke with a heavy heart. The first objects that met her eyes were the chopped-off ends of the bedposts. She groaned to herself. Her mother would be furious. The raw, open wood looked worse to her in the bright morning sunlight than it had the night before. She looked up at the ceiling and tried to convince herself once again that it was worth not having the old canopy hanging above her.

The house was quiet, and she wondered what time it was. She sat up in bed and leaned over to see the small clock on her bureau; it said ten minutes to seven. For a Saturday it was very early. Her father, who usually slept late on Saturday mornings, was probably still asleep, Ethan certainly was, and her mother would undoubtedly also sleep late after last night's dance. If she got up

65

very quietly, maybe she would be lucky enough to get out of the house before anyone else woke up. Then she could escape a big commotion with her mother about the bed first thing in the morning. And even more important, she would not have to hear about last night's dance. She could just see that hurt, accusing look in her mother's eyes as she told her what everyone wore and how pretty the girls were ("no one there was as pretty as you," her mother would say, as if that meant anything!). She would be sure to tell her, too, all about Adam and the lovely girl with him.

Well, she didn't want to hear about it.

Tory lay in bed thinking about where she could go if she got up now. They were always up early in Amy's house, and even if Amy had got home late last night, she would be up by seven. Quietly she slipped out of bed and put on her clothes. A pair of shorts and a shirt and an old pair of sneakers were enough. She tiptoed down the stairs and decided it was safest not to take a chance on stopping for breakfast. Ethan might come down, and then the whole household would be up.

She went out the back door, closing it gently behind her. It was nice being out so early in the morning. The dew on the grass wet her sneakers, but it was a pleasant wetness; it felt the way everything smelled, fresh and earthy. A fat robin flew by, carrying a worm in his mouth, and he looked so pleased with himself that Tory had to laugh.

She sighed with relief as she walked away from her house, feeling like a prisoner who has won an extension of time—a small, extra bit of freedom that she knew she would have to pay for later. But that was later, and now the sun was shining, the birds were singing, and she was free.

Amy and her mother were both in the kitchen when Tory timidly knocked on their back door. "For heaven's sake, what's the matter?" Amy's surprise was quickly replaced by anxiety. "Has anything happened?"

"Not really," Tory said. "I woke up early and felt like getting out of the house. I know it's a terrible time to come over."

"Not at all," Mrs. Pitcher said cordially. "Come in and have a cup of coffee with us." She was busy loading up the family washing machine while Amy was washing a pile of dishes.

"I didn't do them last night," Amy said ruefully. "I wanted to get ready for the dance, and Mom was too tired."

"How was the dance?" Tory asked politely.

Mrs. Pitcher looked at her in surprise. "Weren't you there?"

Tory shook her head. "No. I didn't go."

"But your mother ran it!" She couldn't get over the fact that Tory hadn't gone to her mother's own dance, as she put it.

"Maybe that's why Tory didn't want to go," Amy suggested finally.

Mrs. Pitcher's face was shocked. "That's a funny reason," she said. "I don't understand you kids today. You get all worked up about the strangest things, things that never bothered us when we were young. Because your mother works on a dance is no reason to stay away from it, is it now? Your mother's a wonderful woman, Tory."

"I know. And that's not really the reason I didn't go. Amy said that, not me." Tory felt uncomfortable.

"Well, I guess you came over here because you want to talk to Amy," Mrs. Pitcher said kindly. "Go ahead," she said, "take some cereal and milk out on the back porch; I'll finish the dishes."

Amy thanked her mother gratefully. When the girls were alone she looked at Tory questioningly. "What's the matter? I know something is, I can tell by looking at you."

"Everything's the matter." Tory sighed deeply. "You know it really wasn't because of my mother that I didn't go to the dance—at least not directly. It was because of Adam. There was no one else I felt like going with."

"But he asked you, didn't he? Why *didn't* you go with him?" Amy's gentle brown eyes were on Tory's face.

"You know why! Because he *had* to ask me! My

mother practically pushed him into it. You should have seen his face when he asked me. He looked as if he were walking the plank. Was he ever relieved when I said no! He must have been dying to ask Liz Brooks right from the beginning."

"Maybe," Amy said evasively.

Tory leaned toward Amy. She felt her face flush with embarrassment, but she had to know. "How were they together. . . . I mean, do you think they're going steady?"

"No," Amy said. "I don't know, of course, but I just don't think so."

Tory was silent for a few minutes. "I did something awful last night," she finally confessed. "I hated everyone, so I had to take it out on something. I cut the bedposts off my bed."

"Oh, Tory!" Amy cried with dismay. "That beautiful bed of yours! What did your mother say?"

"I don't know. That's why I left the house so early this morning. I didn't want to be around when she found out. But you know," Tory spoke thoughtfully, "I'm not even sure I'm sorry I did it. Do you think that's terrible?" She looked at Amy soberly.

Amy's face was troubled. "I don't know. It was a lovely bed. I guess it depends on the reason you did it. If it was just to destroy something, then I think that's bad."

"But that wasn't it," Tory said emphatically. "I really don't like that bed. I haven't for ages. I hate my whole room—it isn't me. I want to do it over. Don't you ever feel that you need something that is completely and absolutely your own—that no one else has a part in?"

"You mean that your mother didn't do for you," Amy said astutely. "I don't have the same problem with my mother that you have with yours. Sometimes I think she leaves me alone too much, that I run this house more than she does. With you it's different."

"I know," Tory said glumly.

Both girls were silent for a while. Tory wondered if her mother was up yet, and what might be happening at her house if her mother had gone into her room. It made her feel both frightened and defiant. It's my bed, she thought stubbornly, and I don't care what she says.

"How was the dance?" she asked Amy, just for the sake of saying something.

Amy made a face. "Just like all those dances—dull. They shouldn't let the young kids come to a high-school dance. It ends up with more parents than kids. I wish we had a place of our own that was just for the high-school crowd, where we could do what we want. A teen-age canteen or something like that."

Tory sat up straight. "A teen-age canteen! That's a wonderful idea. I just read an article in a magazine about one. I forget the name of the town, but the high-school kids themselves got one going. They did every-thing. They raised money for it, and they got hold of some old building and painted it and decorated it. It looked marvelous in the pictures."

"But where could we get a building?" Amy asked practically.

"I don't know. . . ." Tory stared at the neat rows of tomatoes and lettuce planted in the Pitchers' back yard. Suddenly she let out a whoop. "Hey!" she cried. "There it is, staring us right in the face." She pointed to a large old carriage house set back almost in the center of the block, behind the Pitchers' yard. "Wouldn't that place be ideal? Remember when they had the firemen's ball there once? It would be perfect."

Amy looked skeptical. "Mrs. Honeycomb owns it. She'd never let us use it. I think she was born in it or something."

"She couldn't have been born in the carriage house," Tory said giggling. "That was part of the stable. But I don't know why we couldn't ask her about it anyway, do you?"

"Are you really serious about this?" Amy asked in surprise.

"Why not? Don't you think it's a good idea? I don't know about you, but I'm sick of being pushed around by all the grownups—my mother especially. They all talk about being permissive and reasonable and understanding their children, but when it comes to letting us *do* anything, they're suspicious as if they expected us to pull out a switch blade any minute!" Tory was pacing around the porch as she talked. "Remember the time I dyed my hair?" She faced Amy with a toss of her head. "You'd think I was a fallen woman, because I wanted to see how I'd look as a platinum blonde. And now there's my bed. My mother's going to treat me like an outcast because I cut off my bedposts. Well, I'm sick of it, and I'd like to show them that we can organize something ourselves and run it. We can, I'm sure of it, and I think it will be wonderful."

Amy was looking at her with admiration. "You should have been a suffragette." Then she started giggling.

"What's so funny?" Tory demanded impatiently.

"You won't like this," Amy said, still laughing. "But you looked just like your mother when you were talking. You toss your head exactly the same way she does when she gets excited about something. You're more like her than you think you are. I bet you could be a great organizer, the way she is."

Tory flushed. "Thanks a lot. I don't want to be a great organizer, heaven forbid! But we *could* do this, Amy, don't you think so?" She looked at her pleadingly.

"I don't know. I suppose we could find out about it. But we couldn't do it alone."

"Let's not get any parents mixed up in it," Tory said with alarm. "Of course, we'd have to get a lot of other kids excited, but I don't think that would be hard. Why don't we go around and at least ask Mrs. Honeycomb about the carriage house? What can we lose?"

"What would we say to her?" Amy asked. "You can't just go up to someone and say 'we'd like to use your carriage house for a teen-age canteen.' "

"Why not?" Tory demanded. "It's standing empty. She's one of the people who're always talking about doing something for the community. Well, here's her chance. Let's call her bluff. Come on, let's go see her."

"Now, this minute?" Amy was dismayed. "Shouldn't we think about it and ask some of the other kids first?"

"What's there to think about? If we don't have a place, we're stymied. What can we lose by asking her? Come on, let's go. It's after nine, and she'll be sure to be home in the morning."

Reluctantly Amy followed Tory into the house. The girls combed their hair and told Mrs. Pitcher they were going out, but they didn't say where they were going. They walked around the block to Mrs. Honeycomb's house. It was large, square, and Victorian, with tall, narrow, shuttered windows and a widow's walk on top of its three stories. It was a forbidding place, surrounded by tall, enveloping trees that gave it a dank, musty atmosphere.

The girls hesitated on the open stoop. "I'm scared," Amy whispered. "Me too," Tory agreed. "But it's only old Mrs. Honeycomb. Can you imagine living alone in this house!"

Timidly Tory lifted the brass knocker on the door. The house was as silent as a grave. Finally they heard footsteps and Mrs. Honeycomb's small voice saying, "Who's there?"

They had to repeat their names a few times before she unbolted the door. When she let them in, however, she greeted them with a gracious air, as if receiving callers at this hour of the morning was an everyday occurrence for her. She was a tiny woman, with an air of elegance about her that matched the ornate curlicues on her heavy Victorian furniture and the spacious, high-ceilinged rooms of her house. She looked like a small, fluttery bird with her blue-white hair, her bright blue eyes, and her sharp little wrinkled features as she darted ahead of them with a swish of her long cotton skirt and a crackle of her starched, pink, ruffled high-necked blouse.

She sat down on a straight, high-backed chair and ordered the girls to sit nearby. "I like to have people close to me," she said charmingly, much too vain to admit that she was hard of hearing.

"Now I know *you*," she said to Tory, "you are Tory Darling, and your mother is someone I am extremely fond of. But I don't believe I know your mother." She turned to Amy with her eyebrows raised questioningly.

"No, I don't think you do," Amy said, sitting very straight. "My mother works and doesn't get around to a lot of meetings." She spoke politely, but there was a small note of defiance in her voice.

Mrs. Honeycomb seemed to be amused. "Working is much more important than meetings," she said calmly. Amy relaxed. "I must give you girls some tea," Mrs. Honeycomb said, jumping up unexpectedly. "I have very fine tea sent to me from England; a new shipment has just arrived and you must taste it."

She vanished from the room before Amy or Tory could say a word. Amy leaned over toward Tory and whispered, "You tell her why we came. She seems to think it's just a social visit. We'll be here all morning. Tell her when she comes back."

In a short while Mrs. Honeycomb came in pushing an elegant tea wagon, laden with a china teapot, tiny blue-and-white cups and saucers, and a dish of fancy iced cakes. It looked like a tea party for four o'clock in the afternoon, not ten o'clock in the morning. She poured the tea as if she were serving royalty, and kept up a steady stream of conversation about her delphiniums, the birthday party that had been given her, and how much she treasured Mrs. Darling's friendship.

Finally, after several dark looks from Amy, Tory gathered up her courage, and when Mrs. Honeycomb paused to pop a cake into her mouth, she spoke up. "You have a very beautiful carriage house," she said quickly. "We were wondering, if you don't use it, whether you would consider letting us fix it up as a place for teen-agers to get together."

Mrs. Honeycomb's blue eyes flashed brightly, but when she finished chewing her cake she said sweetly to Tory, "I'm afraid I didn't quite hear what you said. Would you repeat it, please?"

Tory said her piece all over again.

"Why," Mrs. Honeycomb exclaimed, "that must be your mother's idea! My carriage house for a teen-age— what did you call it?"

"I didn't really call it anything," Tory said, "but it would be called a canteen, I suppose."

"A canteen! Why, we had canteens in the First World War. I was young then, and I used to dance with all the soldiers. We had many gay times. But why didn't your mother come herself to discuss such an enchanting idea?"

Tory's and Amy's eyes met. "It wasn't my mother's idea," Tory said. "As a matter of fact, she doesn't know anything about it. It was our idea, Amy's and mine. We thought that if you would let us use your carriage house, we could fix it up. A bunch of us could paint and decorate it. Then maybe we could run some dances, and little by little raise the money to buy things that all of us would enjoy: a Ping-pong table, perhaps build a stage where we could put on plays, and buy a record player and a television set. It would be wonderful if the young people had a place of their own to go to."

"But who would be responsible?" Mrs. Honeycomb asked in a businesslike voice. Her eyes were sharp in her small, delicate face. "I presume you would have some parents on your committee. Who would they be?" She turned to Amy. "You've been very quiet. You answer me."

Amy gasped. "Well, I don't know. As a matter of fact," she said in a stronger voice, "we hadn't thought about having any parents on our committee. We want to do it ourselves."

"Humph." Mrs. Honeycomb turned to Tory. "What have you got to say?"

"I agree with Amy. I don't think we need any parents," Tory said firmly.

"Don't you think your mother should be on such a committee?" Mrs. Honeycomb asked. "She knows how to organize things like this."

The girls looked at each other helplessly. But Tory shook her head. "No, I don't think we want any parents. We want it to be our project." She returned the elderly woman's gaze evenly. "I guess you won't consider letting us use your place under these conditions." She stood up as if to leave. "Thank you very much, and the tea was lovely."

Amy stood up too. "Thank you, Mrs. Honeycomb," she said.

"Well, you girls aren't shilly-shallying," Mrs. Honeycomb said. "I didn't say I wouldn't let you use the carriage house. My terms are very simple. You must consult with me before you pick a color to paint it, and I will have no parties in the evening without proper chaperons. Is that understood?"

Tory and Amy broke into smiles. "You mean you'll let us have it!" Tory exclaimed. "That's wonderful. Of course, we wouldn't do anything to the building without asking your permission first, and naturally we'd have to have a chaperon for an evening party. Oh, I'm so excited!"

"It's wonderful," Amy cried.

The two girls thanked Mrs. Honeycomb profusely. When she showed them to the door, she unexpectedly kissed each of them on the cheek. "It was lovely having you come to see me this morning. I will enjoy having young people about. It gets very lonesome here sometimes. You must come again. And you," she said turning to Tory, "you have many of the qualities of your mother. You are determined, the way she is. I admire determined women."

Once outside the girls turned to each other excitedly. "She really is a dear," Amy said. "It was easy as pie. You are terrific, Tory," she added.

"I didn't do anything," Tory said. "We just stuck to our guns, that's all. But this bit about my mother, that's twice today. You first and then Mrs. Honeycomb. I don't want to be like my mother—it worries me."

"Maybe you're fighting yourself just as much as your mother," Amy said wisely. "I don't believe you hate your mother as much as you think you do."

"I don't really hate her—sometimes I love her. She just drives me crazy, that's all. Oh, in the excitement I almost forgot. She must have seen my room by now. I guess I'd better go home and face the music. I'll call you later. Now that we really have a canteen, there's a lot we have to do. Imagine, all in one little morning! I *am* excited!" She hugged Amy before she left her at her door and, with her steps slowing down, she went on to her own house.

Chapter 5

TORY's heart beat faster and faster as she neared home. While she was still very excited about the idea of the canteen, the confidence she had felt when she left Mrs. Honeycomb now fled, and she trembled with apprehension at what her mother would say about it.

Tory walked around to the rear of the house, more as a delaying measure than anything else. She picked up the lid of the garbage can, which had fallen to the ground, and carefully placed it back where it belonged. Spying a few tall weeds in her mother's peony bed, she vigorously pulled them out. Then she looked around the yard, but she couldn't think of anything else to do. Hesitantly she went into the kitchen.

Her parents were at the kitchen table having a cup of coffee. "Hello," Tory said tentatively.

"You went out pretty early this morning," her father commented.

"I know. I had breakfast over at Amy's."

She looked everywhere but at her mother, although she could feel her mother's eyes on her. Finally, with dread in her heart, she forced herself to meet her mother's gaze.

"I'm sorry you felt you had to run away this morning," Mrs. Darling said in a low voice, and then, astonishingly, her eyes filled with tears. "Oh Tory, how could you have done such a thing! That beautiful old bed—it just breaks my heart. . . ." Mrs. Darling took out her handkerchief to wipe her eyes; she was visibly trying to control her sobs.

"But it's only a bed, Mother." Tory's face was stricken. "I didn't think it would upset you so much. I'm sorry, really I am."

"You should be sorry," Mr. Darling said crisply. "It was a very destructive thing to do."

"It just hurts me so," Mrs. Darling said between sobs, "to see that bed spoiled. I feel as if Tory had taken a knife and cut me."

"Mother, how can you say such a thing!" Tory was shocked, and she felt anger rising within her. If only she would scold me, she thought desperately, instead of acting hurt. "The bed has nothing to do with you," Tory pleaded, convincing herself of it at that moment.

"I just didn't like it and decided to do something about it."

"A matter like this is for your mother to decide," Mr. Darling said. "This is her home. When you are grown-up and have your own home, you can chop up all the furniture you want, although I hope you will outgrow the need by that time."

"But the bed is mine!" Tory was indignant at the injustice of the accusations against her. "Even Mother has to admit that. You gave it to me for my birthday!"

"If you were a small child and deliberately broke a brand-new toy we'd given you, we'd be equally upset. It doesn't matter who owns the bed, it's a matter of destruction." Mr. Darling's even disposition was being provoked.

"But I wasn't *breaking* something! I was fixing it, changing it to suit my taste," Tory insisted.

"Please don't argue," Mrs. Darling pleaded. "I can't bear arguments. What's done is done. We'll make the best of it. We'll turn your room into one that's completely modern. Isn't that what you want?" Mrs. Darling wiped her tears away and turned a brave face to Tory.

"Oh, Mother!" Tory was near tears now herself. "I don't *know* what I want. I just want to think, to mull it out, to muddle through by myself! I wish you could understand that." Her voice ended on a high, loud note.

"This is hardly the time to start screaming at your mother," Mr. Darling said impatiently. "I think you'd better apologize."

"I'm sorry," Tory said wearily. Why did everything always get so confused? And why was she always in the wrong? She felt discouraged and beaten, as if she could never do anything right. Deliberately she thought about the possibility of the canteen, and some of her natural, buoyant confidence came back. "Amy and I had a marvelous idea this morning," she said suddenly. "We're going to organize a teen-age canteen, and Mrs. Honeycomb said we could use her carriage house. Isn't that wonderful?"

Tory looked from her mother to her father excitedly. "I'm really sorry about the bed," she said to her mother with a swift feeling of remorse, "and I'll fix the room up, Mom, don't worry. You'll see how artistic I am when we start decorating that carriage house. I have some wild ideas already. Isn't that the greatest, though?"

"It sounds like a very ambitious undertaking," Mr. Darling said soberly. "I hope you young people know how to go about it."

"Who is doing this?" Mrs. Darling asked, still drying her eyes.

"So far it's just Amy and me," Tory confessed. "But now that we have the place I guess we'll get hold of some of the others, buy some paint, and start fixing it up."

"But you and a few other youngsters can't organize a teen-age canteen for the town," Mrs. Darling remonstrated. "It takes a lot of planning, a lot of careful thinking. Besides, there will be money involved and someone must be responsible for that."

Tory felt her heart sink again. "There's nothing complicated about it. We'll figure out how to buy the paint and start working. Once we paint the place, the rest will be a cinch. Little by little we'll get the things we need. Isn't Ethan's old record player someplace down in the cellar? I'd like to bring that over."

"I'm afraid it won't run without electricity," Mrs. Darling said. "You see what I mean. You're going to need a lot of help from people with experience. I'm surprised that Mrs. Honeycomb said you could go right ahead. Actually we should have an architect look at that carriage house before you do a thing. It may be unsafe for all we know."

"Mother, that carriage house has been standing for nearly a hundred years. What makes you think it's going to fall apart now? I bet it's better built than this house, isn't it, Daddy?"

"I imagine it's sound," Mr. Darling said, "but your mother's right. She knows about these things. You work it out with her. I have to run along now. Where's Ethan?" he asked Mrs. Darling. "There's a lot we have to do outdoors. I want to move those two small pine trees, they're too crowded, and I thought we might put in some vegetables."

"Ethan's playing outside, waiting for you, dear," she reminded him.

With a sinking heart Tory watched her father disappear outside. She didn't want to be left alone with her mother. She sensed trouble ahead.

"I don't want to butt into your affairs," Mrs. Darling addressed Tory, "but I must say what I believe is right. I think it's foolhardy for a small group of youngsters to try and start from scratch to build and organize a teen-age canteen. It requires money and a great many other things. I'm not even sure Mrs. Honeycomb's carriage house is the best place for the canteen. Shouldn't it be closer to the village, more centrally located? And what about the noise? Won't it bother her? I don't see how Mrs. Honeycomb could have agreed to such an idea! Of course, she's pretty old. . . ."

"Mrs. Honeycomb is not senile, if that's what you're thinking," Tory said. "She knew very well what she was doing. She said she'd love having young people around, they will keep her from being lonesome. Who knows what the problems will be? We'll figure them out as we get to them. There's no sense in being negative! The location's okay, most of the boys drive cars anyway, and it's not that far from the village. We wouldn't want something right in the middle of town, we want some privacy."

"I think I'd better talk to some of the other mothers and see what they think. I don't know Mrs. Pitcher, but I'm going to call her up. Who else did you say you were going to ask?"

"I didn't say. You're going to spoil everything! Why do you have to call other mothers? There's nothing to call them about. Give us a chance, why don't you?"

"Then once it gets started, you'll say it's too late. No," Mrs. Darling said firmly. "I think I'd better take a hand right now."

Tory felt as if she were sinking into quicksand. "Why can't you leave anything alone?" she cried. She was losing her temper, but she didn't care anymore. "This is my affair, not yours," she said furiously. "I wish I hadn't told you about it. I'm a fool to think I can ever tell you anything! You want to take over, to run everything your way. I can't bear it any longer."

Tory ran out of the kitchen and up the stairs to her own room, the sobs choking her throat. She slammed the bedroom door behind her, threw herself on her unmade bed, and let the sobs come. Desperate ideas ran through her head: she would run away and get a job, she would go and live at Amy's, she would never speak to her mother again. . . .

She was filled with hate and despair, and she was frightened by the intensity of her own feelings. Her mind jumped from one extreme to another, first hating herself and then hating her mother; one minute feeling frightened and alone, the next angry and defiant, wanting to fight the whole world. The one thing that she kept coming back to, however, was her determination to show her mother that she *could* do it alone, that she and her friends could get a fine canteen going. If she could succeed in doing that, then nothing her mother could do or say would touch her any more. She would be someone in her own right, a person her mother would have to respect.

With a new surge of energy she hastily made her bed and straightened up her room. Then she went flying back to Amy's house, so that the two of them could make plans.

The girls made up a list of teen-agers who they thought would be interested in the canteen and who would work for it. They called a meeting for the following week, after the high-school graduation, when school would be over for the summer. Even though Amy's house was smaller than Tory's, they agreed it would be better to meet there for Tory wanted to steer clear of her family.

The week went by quickly, as the last week of school

usually does. The main thing on Tory's mind was the canteen, and she thought about it constantly. She didn't know if her mother had made any of her threatened phone calls. She had heard her talking to Mrs. Harris, but since nothing further was said, she decided to forget about it.

Adam was one of the boys invited to the meeting, and one evening, after her parents had gone out, Tory found herself alone with him. She was filled with all her ideas, and she started telling him about them. They were sitting in the kitchen, and Tory was putting off doing the dishes. The pink glow of the June twilight filled the room and gave a remarkable, theatrical light to Adam's dark, sun-tanned face. He sat across the kitchen table from her, leaning on his elbows, his chin resting on his hands, and he watched her face intently.

"I want the inside to be very dramatic," Tory said. "I think some of it might be whitewashed, and perhaps one of the big walls painted a dark red or a murky olive green. Wouldn't that be stunning?"

Adam nodded his head silently.

"And I think we can put up a stage at the far end. It's wide enough for a fairly good-sized one with wings, and when we have the money we can buy a real curtain. At dances the orchestra can play from the stage, so we'll have the whole floor for dancing. There's a partitioned-off room near the entrance, where they used to keep saddles and bridles, that we can make into a game room with a Ping-pong table, a dart board, and stuff. And we ought to have a kitchen. . . ."

"You have it all figured out," Adam commented. "Why do you want a committee? Why don't you just tell everyone what to do?"

"What do you mean?" Tory stared at him uneasily. Was he serious or was he fooling?

"I mean you're such an organizer. I didn't think you had it in you. You act quiet and shy, but you're really the aggressive type." He said it good-naturedly, but there was a knowing smile on his face that hit Tory hard. She burned with indignation.

"That's not a very nice thing to say. Just because I have ideas doesn't mean I'm aggressive. I'm not pushing anyone around."

"Are you sure?" Adam asked with a grin, but his eyes were serious. "I have a feeling no one had better stand in your way, that's all. Maybe I'm wrong."

"Well, I'll fight for what I believe in," Tory said. "Do you consider that being aggressive?"

"I don't know. I guess it depends on how you fight and whether you believe in the right things or not. But you don't like anyone else to fight, do you?"

"What do you mean by that?" Tory demanded.

"Well, you don't like pushy people, but I notice you push when you want to," Adam said.

"You make me sound like some kind of an ogre," Tory said with a grimace.

A little later Adam got up and left. He had offered to stay and help Tory with the dishes, but she refused. She felt strangely uncomfortable when she was alone with him. He was critical of her, and she longed to have him like her. Again and again she had the frightening desire that he kiss her. She needed to have him reaffirm her femininity and dismiss the fears about herself and her mother that were becoming all entwined in one. Instead he made her feel so self-conscious that it was almost a relief when he left.

But what he had said stayed with her. Whom did he think she was pushing around? Suddenly it occurred to her that he must have heard her arguing with her mother. But her mother was the aggressive one, Tory thought angrily. That was exactly the right word for her mother! Behind all that sweet, soft femininity she was really hard and aggressive; she ruled the whole household, including her husband. Didn't Adam see that? Was he taken in by her mother too, along with everyone else?

Tory worked herself up into a very unhappy state of mind. Adam's teasing words confused and angered her, yet something she herself had said rang a familiar note. "I'll fight for what I believe in"—wasn't that one of her mother's favorite expressions? Tory thought about herself with alarm. *Was she like her mother?* But it couldn't be; the things her mother believed in and spent so much time fussing about were so trivial to Tory! While she. . . . Her thoughts broke off in dismay. Was she acting out of a selfish motive, organizing the canteen mainly as a chance to show her mother what she could do? Yet the canteen was in itself a very good thing. . . .

It was very difficult to know what was really right, and what she truly believed in. But she didn't want to be an aggressive woman, that much she was sure of. She wanted to be charming and feminine and look up to a man, the way she admired Adam. He acted so grown-up and sure of himself, so independent. His father was dying, everyone seemed to know that, but on the out-side Adam remained quiet and serene. He had worked just as hard in school, and now he had a summer job with a construction gang.

He had started work a few days ago and had told her mother that he probably wouldn't eat with them any more. Mrs. Darling had coaxed him to continue, but he had said that in the summer he could manage at home very well.

Tory realized with a pang that she might not see him once he stopped coming over for his dinners. She was sure he never told Liz Brooks that *she* was aggressive. Tory felt so miserable she was almost ready to give up

the canteen now, before it even got started. If she had
any sense, she thought, she'd go downstairs and call
Amy and suggest that they both forget the whole thing.

Yet a stubborn streak in her argued that this would
be a foolish, weak thing to do, and would prove nothing. She would show her mother and Adam both that
she could organize something without being pushy and
aggressive. She was sure it could be done and that she
could do it.

On Monday night they had a very good turnout for
the meeting at Amy's house. Adam came, Amy's boy
friend Woodie, and the Sutton boys, two brothers Don
and Gary. Helen Fisher turned up, as well as Liz
Brooks, the Hanson twins, and Eileen Bancroft, whose
father was president of the bank.

Amy and Tory explained what it was all about, and
Amy made a motion that Tory be chairman. Tory said
she thought it would be better if someone else were,
but secretly she was very flattered and pleased.

"It was Tory's idea," Amy said, "and she should be
chairman." She was elected unanimously.

Next came the question of how to raise the money to
buy paint, lumber for the stage, and to pay for the
necessary carpentry work and installing a kitchen. Liz
Brooks, who looked exactly like a pretty kitten about
to pounce on a ball of wool, suggested that they have a
dance.

"But a dance is a lot of work," Tory argued. "We'll use up all our time and energy on it instead of fixing up the place."

Helen Fisher, a tall, forceful girl, backed up Liz. "But a dance is fun; everyone likes dances and everyone will come. We can make a lot of money."

Adam wanted to know if anyone had any other ideas. He looked directly at Tory. "Perhaps you have some other suggestion."

Tory felt as if she were being challenged. She thought quickly. "We have to send out a letter to everyone in the high school, telling them about our idea and asking them to come in and help. Why don't we ask everyone to donate fifty cents at the same time?" Tory looked around the circle of faces to judge their reaction. Amy was nodding her head in approval, and so were Eileen Bancroft and the boys. Liz looked undecided as did the twins, and Helen Fisher registered disapproval.

"I don't think we should ask people for money," Helen said. "We'll never get it. People want something for their money."

"They'll have a canteen, isn't that something?" Amy protested.

"But a letter will cost money," Adam remarked. "Who will pay for it?"

"We can all chip in, can't we?" Eileen suggested.

"Maybe *you* can," Woodie said matter-of-factly. "I don't know about the rest of us, it depends how much."

"Let's come to order," Tory said sharply, seeing the unhappy expression on Eileen's face. "I can get a letter mimeographed down at my father's office. Maybe Eileen can lend us the money for the postage, and we can pay her back when the donations come in. But who should write the letter?"

"I don't think we should send a letter," Helen said vehemently. "We haven't voted on it. Let's vote before we talk about who should write it."

"That's right," Tory agreed. "Someone should make a motion." She felt worried that she wasn't conducting the meeting properly, the way her mother would have done.

"I move that we send out a letter to everyone in the high school asking them to work on the canteen and to contribute fifty cents for materials," Don Sutton said.

"Or maybe it should be fifty cents for membership," Tory said suddenly. "How about that?"

"That's a great idea," Adam said.

"I don't think so," Amy disagreed. "How much to pay for membership is an important decision. That should come later, when we have more people and can elect regular officers. And maybe we'll need bylaws, I don't know."

"She's right," Woodie said approvingly. "Let's just ask for donations now, and worry about membership later."

"Call the question," Gary called out.

Tory asked for a show of hands, and the motion was passed, with Helen Fisher looking disgruntled and voting against it alone.

"But what about the kitchen?" Woodie asked. "That's going to be expensive. I think we should canvass the dealers in town and see if they will donate used equipment." The others agreed that the suggestion was wonderful, and the boys were assigned to follow through on it.

Adam and Tory were asked to draft the letter and to show it to as many of the others as possible for approval. They decided to meet again a week later at Eileen's house, when the letter would be mimeographed and ready to send. They would address the envelopes and mail them that night.

The meeting broke up. Adam stayed on after the others left and arranged to meet with Tory the next evening to work on the letter.

"You see, I was right," Adam said to Tory. "You're a born organizer!" Tory wasn't sure whether he meant to compliment her or to tease her. She decided to take the remark as a compliment. "Thank you," she said. "I hope I did everything all right."

"Just like a politician. You know how to get your own way." Adam spoke in a teasing voice, but his eyes studied Tory's face. The color flooded her sun-tanned cheeks. Now she felt that Adam had more on his mind than innocent teasing; she sensed a critical, questioning look in his eyes as if he was trying to make a decision about her.

"I wasn't trying to get my own way. I just didn't agree with Helen. What's wrong with that?" Tory demanded, her eyes flashing.

"Nothing," Adam said placidly. "I was only interested in the way you maneuvered things."

"Well, you agreed with me," Tory said defiantly. "If you didn't, you should have said so!"

"I'm not disagreeing with you now," Adam said. "What are you so excited about?"

"I'm not excited," Tory stated flatly.

After Adam had left, Tory felt very dissatisfied, as if they'd had a fight, or even worse. Adam's implied criticism of her made her feel miserable, and she didn't think it was fair. "I think Adam is really getting to hate me," she said disconsolately to Amy.

"You're nutty," Amy said good-naturedly. "He doesn't hate you. I think he likes you, but I think there's something bothering him."

"What?" Tory asked intently. "Has he said anything to you? Please tell me."

Amy shook her head. "He hasn't said a word, but I have a feeling he has some peculiar notion in his head. He may think you're snobbish."

"Me, snobbish?" Tory was aghast.

"Maybe he thinks you didn't go to the dance with him because he was the poor boy your mother was feeding. Did you ever think of that?"

Tory was close to tears. "He couldn't think that! Do you think he did? Amy, do you? Please tell me the truth."

"Well, I can see how he might be touchy about your not going to the dance with him," Amy said thoughtfully. "I think you should have been more sensitive to his feelings, instead of being wrapped up in your own."

"Amy, will you tell me the truth? Do you think I push people around to get my own way?" Tory's face was miserable as she looked at Amy. Her eyes filled with tears.

"My telling you the truth isn't going to solve anything," Amy said astutely. "I admire the way you stand up for what you want. Frankly, I think it's *how* you do things that matters. Your mother acts so sweet that people never think of her as aggressive. I bet even your father doesn't. But you're more blunt about what you think."

"But isn't that better?" Tory demanded. "It's that sweetness of my mother's that I can't bear. I keep wanting to shout to people that she's not really like that at all. I guess that's why I'm just the opposite. I don't want to be sweet and diplomatic. I think it's awful."

"That's up to you. Then I guess you'll have to face the consequences. You may scare some people off, like Adam."

Tory sighed deeply. "It's hard to figure out what kind of person you want to be."

"That's because you're reacting to your mother," said Amy. "If you got straight about her, you could be yourself and stop worrying."

Tory thought that over for a few minutes. "But I can't help it. I *do* react, so what can I do?"

Amy shrugged her shoulders. "I don't know. But you'll be all right. Don't worry."

"Yes, I'll be a great old maid," Tory said unhappily. "No man will come near me."

"Don't be silly. I think Adam really likes you, but he needs encouragement."

"I don't know how to encourage him," Tory confessed. "I don't know how to be clingy and feminine and fall all over a boy. It makes me sick."

"You don't have to go from one extreme to another," Amy suggested.

Tory left Amy's in a very unhappy frame of mind. When she arrived home she found her mother striding up and down the living room with a piece of paper in her hand. There were some notes on it, which she was obviously trying to memorize.

"What's all this about?" Tory asked idly.

"It's my speech for the Chamber of Commerce, my acceptance speech. Just a few extemporaneous words."

"Not very extemporaneous, if you're memorizing them," Tory commented.

"I'll act as if I'm talking on the spur of the moment. It's better to have it planned and rehearsed."

Tory stared at her mother in amazement. "You don't miss a trick, do you?"

"I don't want to get up and make a fool of myself stammering." Her mother started reading. "Honored Chairman, ladies, and gentlemen. I don't know how to express my pleasure at being here. Although I know little about making speeches, what I say comes from the heart. . . ."

Tory sighed deeply and walked away. Why couldn't people be simple and honest and uncomplicated? She felt sick about Adam and sure that she was losing him completely. At the bottom of her misery, she couldn't help but blame her mother and wish, unhappily, that her life was different.

Chapter 6

THE summer went speeding by. It seemed to Tory that one day the countryside was lush with daisies and wild lilies; the lawns were a smooth, even green. Then overnight the leaves began to turn, and patches of brown replaced the green.

Tory felt as if she had spent the entire vacation immersed in buckets of paint, scrubbing herself with turpentine and going about with long lists of *Things to Do* in her hand. It hadn't been like summer at all. She had hardly ever gone to the beach, she had not set foot on a tennis court, and she had worn practically none of her pretty summer clothes. She had lived in a pair of old shorts and sneakers, suitable for working on the canteen, and when she came home at night she was usually too tired to do anything more than take a shower and read or play records until she fell asleep. Her social life was nil.

"It's the oddest summer I've ever lived through," she said to Amy. It was a hot, muggy night early in September, a week before school opened. The girls were sitting in the Pitchers' garden, too hot to go inside, yet tormented by the bugs. They kept dousing themselves with insect repellent, even though, as Amy pointed out, the smell seemed to bother them more than it did the bugs.

"I've hardly gone out on a date the whole summer," Tory said with a sigh.

"I know." Amy nodded her head. "What's with you and Adam?"

Tory shrugged her shoulders. "Nothing, I guess. He comes around to the canteen week ends, when he's not working, but I haven't seen him alone in ages. I suppose he takes out Liz Brooks."

"I don't think so," Amy said. "I still think he likes you, but that something peculiar happened between you."

"Something peculiar seems to have happened between me and a few other people this summer," Tory commented. "My mother and I have been battling constantly all summer long."

Tory stared glumly into the night. She was tired. The summer had been an arduous one, and she had

often wondered why she had ever begun on the canteen in the first place. It had started off with a bang.
The high-school crowd had responded to the idea with
enormous enthusiasm, and for the first few weeks everyone wanted to work. The fifty-cent pieces had come
rolling in, and the painting had gone on at a furious
pace. But then other things interfered: some people
went away on vacations, others took jobs, and some just
got bored.

Tory found that as chairman she had to keep after
everyone constantly in order to get the work finished.
When she wasn't working herself, she had to round up
workers on the telephone and dream up new ideas to
keep them interested. The major part of the work fell
upon a small core of the faithful: Helen Fisher, who
fought about everything, but who worked nevertheless;
Amy, when she could leave home or bring the younger
kids along with her; the twins; and Tory. Woodie and
Adam were willing to work, but they could come only
on week ends or after work at five o'clock. The others
appeared sporadically, usually when word got around
that a party would be held.

The place was almost finished by now, but Tory was
discouraged and exhausted, and very apprehensive
about the gala opening planned for three weeks later.
They were arranging a round of festivities: an open
house and tea on Saturday afternoon for the commu-

nity in general, a play Saturday night, and a dance afterward. On Sunday the canteen would be open the first day for its members. They could use it any time between three in the afternoon and ten in the evening, to play records and dance, for Ping-pong or cards, or just to sit around and talk.

Tory was positive it would all be a total flop. She was sure that no one would turn up, and if they did, the tea would be a mess, the play a failure, and the dance a shambles.

It also seemed to Tory that no matter how she had tackled a particular job, or what her ideas were, some-how or other her mother had gently managed to make a countersuggestion. Tory found this unbearable, and she was convinced that her mother was getting back at her for having kept her committees and organizations away from the canteen. As a result, each time Tory ran into difficulties in her job as chairman, she took it both as a personal challenge and more grist for her mother's mill. This had all been very wearing.

Tory had tried to make her phone calls while her mother was out of the house and to keep her from knowing about the heartbreaking problems she ran into. But it had been a hopeless situation. Mrs. Darling seemed to know anyway when things went wrong and she felt hurt when Tory ignored her suggestions. The upshot of it was that Tory avoided any discussion about the canteen with her mother, which only made matters worse.

Then there was the matter of Adam. Tory was always aware of a current of attraction between them whenever they were near each other, but she was also aware of a feeling of mistrust. They were like two people who had once walked down a sunny street together, hand in hand and happy in each other's company. Then suddenly the sun clouded over and they lost each other. Ever since they had been trying to get back to the sunlight, but their suspicions of each other kept them apart.

She could not get interested in anyone else. A look from Adam's dark eyes, the toss of his head, or even a scowl on his face meant more to her than she dared to think. And the more she longed to be near him and for his attention, the more she blamed her mother for the strain between them. She dated their break from the time he started coming to their house for dinner, and she could never forgive her mother for arranging it.

As Tory thought morosely about the summer, wishing she could be more enthusiastic about the forthcoming opening of the canteen, Mrs. Pitcher came home and sat outside with the girls.

"Mrs. Harris called me from the P.T.A. today." Mrs. Pitcher turned to Tory. "Your mother's got the Chamber of Commerce to invite a group of foreign boys and girls to visit Squash Hollow, and the P.T.A.'s trying to find places for them to stay for the week end."

"Sounds like my mother," Tory said. "I suppose we'll have a bunch of them at our house—to see the typical American family at work and play. She does get the wildest ideas! The poor kids will probably be bored to death from being toted around by the Chamber of Commerce, and everyone will have a hideous week end."

"I hope not," Mrs. Pitcher said. "It's the week end your canteen is opening. That's the whole idea of it, so that foreign students can see how young people get together in this country, can see their social life and what they do."

Tory sat up straight now. "She invited them for the week end of our opening?" she asked unbelievingly. "You're kidding! She couldn't do that! We're all going to be so busy, we can't possibly entertain a bunch of foreign kids. Besides. . . ." Tory was white with anger.

"I think she figured the activities at the canteen would entertain them," Mrs. Pitcher said mildly.

"But it makes me mad. Why didn't she discuss it with us at the canteen first?" Tory demanded. "She's the one who always says everything must be done in an organized way. She wants us to discuss every move with her—or the Chamber of Commerce or the P.T.A.—and now she goes off and does this on her own!"

"She's not doing it alone, she's acting for the Chamber of Commerce; it's part of her job as Mother of the Year. Maybe someone there thought of it."

"I know my mother. She thought of it." Tory bit her lower lip nervously to control her temper. She knew she was absurd to get so angry, and that it was part of her touchiness about her mother, but she couldn't help it. This was the last straw. She was ashamed of her thoughts, but it occurred to her that her mother was deliberately trying to interfere with the canteen's opening week end and spoil it for Tory. "Why couldn't she keep out of it!" Tory said aloud. "She always has to meddle with everything!"

"She's not meddling," Mrs. Pitcher said patiently. "The Chamber of Commerce thought it would be a good opportunity to invite some foreign students to visit, and really, Tory, I think it will help the canteen. It will provide an added note, some extra excitement, and you'll get a bigger crowd. You should be glad of that."

"That's true, Tory," Amy said. "It will bring a bigger crowd. I think it will be fun."

"I hope so," Tory said unenthusiastically. "We'll see."

When Tory came home that evening, Mrs. Darling was fluttering with excitement. In between telephone calls she tried to tell Tory about the young foreign students coming to visit Squash Hollow. "We're not sure yet how many there will be. . . ." She spoke to Tory while she was dialing a number, and then Tory had to wait while she had a long, involved telephone conversation with someone about whether they would like a girl or a boy staying with them. Mrs. Darling warned them at the end of her call that their visitor might be "quite black."

"Why do you have to tell them their guest is going to be dark," Tory demanded indignantly, when her mother had hung up.

"I think people have to know," Mrs. Darling said. "I don't want any embarrassment."

"It sounds all wrong to me," Tory insisted. "If they want to entertain a guest, they do, and what color skin the guest has doesn't matter."

"That's how you and I feel, Tory, but not everyone looks at it that way, unfortunately," Mrs. Darling said placidly. "You're very idealistic."

"I don't think so. And I think you're hypocritical. You invite all these kids here to show them how democracy works, but you have to go around warning everyone they might have a colored guest! You wouldn't explain that a guest has blue eyes and blond hair, why do you have to say anything about the color of his skin?" Tory knew she was in the mood to pick a fight with her mother, but she was also convinced of the sincerity of what she was saying.

"People aren't prejudiced against blue eyes and blond hair," Mrs. Darling said with alacrity. "Unfortunately, many people do have prejudices against dark-skinned people. I cannot change the world overnight, and I don't want any young guest to be embarrassed or any household taken by surprise. Now I have a lot of phoning to do, but if you're interested, I'd like to tell you about our plans." Mrs. Darling faced Tory across the hall table, where she sat with the telephone in front of her. She had a list of names that she had been checking off as she called.

"Thanks a lot for cuing me in," Tory said. "I think you should have consulted us before you invited a bunch of strange kids for the opening of the canteen."

"I don't see that it affects the canteen one bit," Mrs. Darling said. "Aren't you glad they're coming? Talk about democracy and being hypocritical, I should think you'd welcome a chance to entertain some young people from foreign countries. And it will give you a chance to show off your canteen."

"How many are coming?" Tory asked.

"We're not sure yet. We hope about ten or twelve. Some people at Yale are arranging it for us. A few may be from prep schools, but most of them will be college students. And they're from all over, from Ghana, Nigeria, India, Holland, England, Norway . . . isn't it exciting?" Mrs. Darling's eyes were shining.

"It's going to be boring," Tory said flatly. "Everyone will be self-conscious and formal. It's one of those gestures that sounds great, but turns out to be awful. What are we going to learn about each other in a week end, and especially one that's so crowded already?"

"Really, Tory, I hope you don't talk that way at the canteen. It *will* be a flop if you decide to make it one. I am extremely disappointed in your attitude. I thought that at least as chairman of the canteen, you would welcome this."

"As chairman of the canteen, you might have discussed this with me first," Tory said stonily.

She and her mother stared at each other uncomfortably. "I hope," Mrs. Darling said, "that you will do everything you can to make the week end a successful one."

"Oh, of course I will," Tory said impatiently. "What do you take me for? But I have a right to tell you what I think, haven't I?"

"I suppose so," Mrs. Darling said wearily. "But sometimes I think I've brought you up all wrong. Perhaps it was better in the old days when children were seen but not heard."

"That's a fine thing to say," Tory declared. "You wouldn't like me to be a ninny, would you? And besides, when children were seen and not heard mothers didn't have the freedom you have, either," Tory said victoriously.

"I'm not so sure freedom is the right word," Mrs. Darling murmured. She paused and then added, "I was going to ask you to clean up the sleeping porch. I thought we could put a boy out there. Then we can move the folding cot into your room for one of the girls. How would that be?"

"I suppose it'll be all right," Tory said. She didn't say anything aloud, but the idea of having a totally strange girl from a foreign country share her room with her was not very appealing. She felt it was an invasion of her privacy, especially on a week end when at moments she would want to go to her room, close the door, and shut out the rest of the world. With a sinking heart, Tory thought about how odd her room would look to a stranger. Now that the canopy was gone and the bedposts were sawed off, the dainty frilliness of the rest of the room looked grotesque. The foreign girl would get a very peculiar idea of a typical American home, Tory thought ruefully.

As the week end of the canteen's opening came nearer, Tory became more and more apprehensive. Physically, the carriage house had turned out most successfully. One area had been left as a makeshift auditorium, with space for dancing and a simple stage built at one end of it. They had whitewashed the two side walls up to ten feet, leaving the natural-aged wood above in its original state. The beams and the lofty roof of the old house were left exposed. The stage was made mostly out of old timbers, and the wall facing the stage was a dark red. Partitions had been put up dividing off smaller rooms: the kitchen, one for games, one for music, and a general entranceway with a place for coats. Furniture had been collected from various homes, and for the opening week end they borrowed folding chairs from the two churches in town to seat people for the play. They hoped to make enough money from it to buy their own chairs and some other necessities.

Tory had terrible nightmares about having everything ready and nobody showing up. And every time she watched a rehearsal of the one-act play they were putting on, it looked worse to her. She was sure everyone would forget their parts, and it would all be a mess.

Visiting students were the final blow. While she kept nodding her head to everyone, apparently agreeing that the students' visit was marvelous, privately she and Amy were both convinced they would turn out to be the world's worst drips. "You can just imagine the kind of kids who would want to do this," Tory said to Amy. "They're probably real bookworms, who never have any fun at all."

"I'm sure of it," Amy agreed. "All economics majors no doubt."

The fateful Friday finally came. When Tory got home from school, the two young guests who were to stay at the Darling house had arrived. At noon Mrs. Darling and a group from the Chamber of Commerce and the P.T.A. had met twelve young people and escorted them to their various host homes. Tory had rushed home feeling apprehensive about the week end and troubled by the added worry of having strangers to entertain. She felt nervous and uneasy as she entered her own front door.

The sight that met her eyes almost made her giggle; it was so exactly the worst that she had expected. There in her living room were three people, her mother, a boy, and a girl. Tory had never seen three people look more uncomfortable in her whole life. They were all sitting very straight and looked as relaxed as if they were waiting in a dentist's office to have their teeth pulled out.

The boy and girl, clearly from India, were beautiful to look at; they looked like brother and sister. The girl was dressed in a native sari, a lovely blue-and-gold woven thing. She had a little black caste mark on her forehead and wore small gold earrings that tinkled when she moved her head. The boy, dressed in western clothes, was light-skinned like the girl, with straight, even features and large, dark, almost sad eyes.

The young people stood up when Tory came in, and her mother introduced them: Santha Srivastava and her brother Ravi from New Delhi. They greeted Tory in a polite and formal fashion. Their voices were soft, and they spoke English beautifully with a British accent.

Tory sat down on the settee next to her mother and wondered what to talk about. The conversation went on in a desultory fashion. Tory, feeling like a fool, asked the typical cliché questions about how they liked America, where they went to school, and so forth. They answered politely, and, in turn, asked Tory similar questions.

Santha was in her first year of a junior college and had only arrived in America last summer. Ravi, who was a few years older, was a sophomore in college and had been away from home since his freshman year. He was planning to major in engineering. They both said they found America most interesting and that they liked it very much.

How are we ever going to get through this week end! Tory thought. It's going to be ghastly, with all of us sitting around looking foolish and being polite to each other, just waiting for the week end to come to an end.

Her mother was making general conversation when

Santha turned to Tory and asked in a soft, shy voice, "Do you have a boy friend you go steady with?"

Tory laughed and said no, she didn't. Santha laughed too and said she thought that all pretty American girls went steady. That broke the ice. Santha and Tory began talking in a more intimate fashion, and when Mrs. Darling got up and excused herself a short while later, Ravi said he would love to hear some good American jazz records.

Tory was delighted and put a stack of records on her record player. Before long Tory found herself dancing with Ravi, who turned out to be a beautifully smooth dancer, while Santha watched them with delight.

Suddenly Tory looked up and found his dark eyes scrutinizing her face very seriously. She felt herself tremble slightly under the steadiness of his gaze, but she asked lightly, "What's the matter? Am I doing something wrong?"

Ravi shook his head. "No. I am just trying to make sure I am not dreaming. This is something I have thought about very often—long before I ever came to the United States. And now it is really happening to me. I am really here in a typical American town, in a typical American home, and I am dancing informally with a very pretty American girl. It is not a ball, there are no chaperons, we are simply having a jolly time together. You cannot know what this means to me."

Tory was tremendously moved by the way Ravi spoke and the emotion on his face. She felt terribly ashamed of her own misgivings about the week end, realizing the full impact of what this visit meant to Ravi and Santha. Perhaps her mother was right. They *did* have little opportunity to visit casually in an American home. She thought with a pang of sympathy how hard it must be for them, so many thousands of miles from their own friends and family, meeting strangers constantly, having to be on their best behavior, and learning new ways all the time.

She found herself relaxing in Ravi's arms, and in no time he was twirling her around like a professional dancer, her feet flying. They stopped breathlessly to change records; Tory's eyes met Ravi's, and they both laughed. Ravi was very good-looking; his face was gay now, and his sad eyes were no longer sad but smiling. Tory felt a daring excitement within her. She hadn't felt like this in ages—perhaps never before. It was different from the feeling she had for Adam, which was warm and deep and close; this was almost a recklessness, a challenge, wanting Ravi to like her, wanting him to have the impression of an American girl that would be the best that she could make it, wanting to make this week end something significant and important, something that Ravi would remember all his life.

And, Tory thought, her spirits rising up to the

clouds, perhaps it will be a week end that I shall never forget either.

Later, when her mother came in and casually announced that she had invited Adam to dinner that night, Tory was amazed by her own reaction. Automatically, she first thought, heavens, there she goes again, my meddling mother! But then she thought, it will be good to have a fourth. Also, she realized a bit self-consciously, it wouldn't hurt for Adam to see how attentive Ravi, a handsome college sophomore, was to her. "That's great," she said to her mother. "I'm glad you asked him over."

Her mother gave her a somewhat startled look, but she didn't say anything.

As far as Tory was concerned the evening was a huge success. Ravi never left her side. His eyes were constantly on her, as though, if he turned away for a moment, she might vanish into thin air and never come back. Santha gave her attention to Adam, but Tory was aware of his searching glances every now and then, even while he seemed to be engrossed in conversation. Every once in a while, perhaps while she was dancing with Ravi, she found Adam looking at her, as if there were many questions in his mind that needed answering. She wanted to run across to him, to hold his face between her hands, and to tell him that she loved him and that everything would be all right. But instead she went on flirting with Ravi and enjoying it immensely.

At the end of the evening, after they had gone into the kitchen and eaten dozens of melted cheese sandwiches and consumed large quantities of soda, Tory decided it had been the nicest evening she had spent the entire summer. And she enjoyed sharing her room with Santha and talking to her about the evening.

The two girls talked about many things. In a burst of confidence Tory explained to Santha why her room looked such a mess. "I want to do it my own way, but I just haven't got around to it," Tory ended up. "Or perhaps I haven't got the courage, or I don't know how I really want it."

Santha smiled sympathetically. "But you are so lucky," she said, "with the freedom you have. In my country, women cannot do the things you do here. Or the many things your mother does. You should be very happy."

"I guess we all think the grass is greener across the way," Tory said wistfully. "I have often thought how nice it would be to have an old-fashioned mother, who stayed home and took care of the house, and didn't do a lot of other things. I think I'd like to be just a housewife when I get married."

Santha laughed gaily. "You are very funny. I do not know you very well, but I tell you, you would hate it.

You have too much vitality, too many brains. You are like your mother—you want to be busy and to do a great many things!"

"I'm not like my mother at all." Tory shook her head emphatically. "We're completely different."

Santha shrugged her shoulders. "Perhaps, but I think not. Your mother is very charming, she is so very American. Just what I imagined an American woman would be like. And you will be just like her, you wait and see. You are both leaders."

Tory sighed in the darkness. Santha did not know that she was not complimenting Tory. She wondered if Santha, with her wise face and her feminine intuition, was unconsciously giving her a warning note of truth.

If she really was like her mother, what was she hating and fighting so much?

Chapter 7

SATURDAY dawned clear and beautiful. It was one of those perfect days in September when the air is cool and dry, rich with the smell of apples and burning leaves.

It was fun to have Santha in the room beside her, Tory thought, when she opened her eyes. When they got dressed, she watched closely while Santha showed her how she draped her sari over her blouse. "It's beautiful and graceful," Tory said, slipping into her shorts. "You're such a lady in it. But don't you sometimes want to kick it off and run?"

Santha laughed. "I envy you the way you go around, but I would die of embarrassment if I showed my legs that way. Besides, they are not as slim and pretty as yours."

When the girls came downstairs for breakfast, Ravi

was already at the table. This morning he was wearing Indian dress, a homespun white shirt and loose white trousers, and he looked magnificent. "I see you're going native," Santha said to her brother teasingly. "I thought you wanted to be a *real* American!"

"I do," Ravi said. "But I thought I'd let everyone see that there are other ways of dressing."

"What *is* a real American?" Santha asked, turning to Tory. "I keep hearing about the typical American, but I don't think I know yet what he is."

"That's because there is no such animal," Tory said. She remembered the girl on the magazine cover, who had annoyed her so much in the beginning of the summer. "There is a romantic concept of the typical American girl: long-legged, even-featured, well-dressed, beautifully groomed. But there are just as many American girls who are short and fat as there are tall and thin, and there are millions who never see the inside of a beauty parlor, and thousands and thousands with dark skins. So what's a real American?"

"I think what people mean is a kind of personality, not just looks," Ravi said.

"Yes, I know." Tory nodded her head. "A typical American girl, or boy too, I guess, is supposed to be a good sport, interested in athletics, outgoing, intelligent, poised, and sure of herself. I don't know where people get these ideas! It makes me laugh. Most girls I know are not particularly good sports, they go in for athletics to please the boys, and while they may be intelligent, most of them don't have much self-confidence."

"But they don't seem that way to us," Santha said. "To a foreigner, they do seem very good-looking and well-dressed and sure of themselves. Maybe if you traveled in other countries you'd see what we mean. I haven't seen much of America, but I know you don't have the poverty here that a lot of other countries have."

"As there is in our country," Ravi said. "You have never been to India, have you?"

"I've never been out of the United States," Tory confessed.

"You must come sometime. You come with me next spring, when I go home for a few months. Then you will see how things are in my country. I will show you a great deal."

"That would be nice," Tory said laughingly. "After breakfast I'll show you our village. There's nothing much to see, but it's considered a very beautiful New England town."

When they finished breakfast Tory took her guests down to Main Street. Santha and Ravi were interested in everything. They wanted to know why there was a cannon on the green and what it represented. Tory was ashamed that she didn't know, except that it had been there ever since she could remember, and it probably had been put up to commemorate the local unit in World War II.

Tory's guests were entranced with walking through the supermarket. Santha had not yet been in one. "But they have *everything!*" she exclaimed at the well-stocked shelves. "Just look at all those mixes! My goodness, a housewife could make a different cake every day of the year. The women in our villages wouldn't believe that such abundance exists. And it all looks so beautiful. Look, frozen pizza pie, can you imagine such a thing?" She was pulling Ravi from one thing to another, like a large, graceful bird, swooping from tree to tree. "And frozen pink lemonade . . . what makes it pink I wonder? Oh my, I wish my mother could see this!"

It was a new experience for Tory to see everything through Santha's wide, amazed eyes. All the things she had never even noticed or had taken for granted: sixteen different varieties of canned beans, thirty-four different kinds of pickles (Santha counted them excitedly), one entire aisle filled with soaps and detergents for housecleaning, and the frozen foods. Santha simply couldn't get over them; she exclaimed over each one she saw. Tory tried to imagine the difference between the women in Santha's country and the casually dressed, efficient young women surrounding them in the supermarket, unthinkingly stuffing their carts with what Santha called bags of pure gold.

"The children in our country don't know what desserts mean," Santha said sadly. "They are hungry all the time."

"When you come visit our country, we'll take you to see the villages. Things are improving, it is getting better all the time," Ravi said proudly.

"You talk as if I were really coming over to India," Tory said with a smile. "It's very far away."

"It's no farther for us to come to America than for you to come to India. Of course you will come, why not?" Ravi asked the question as if India were a town no more than fifty miles away.

"For one thing, it's very expensive. Not all Americans are rich, you know," Tory said.

Ravi was unperturbed. "We will work something out. My father is with the government back home, and he also has connections with the airlines. Maybe it will cost you nothing. You will be our guest." He spoke simply and matter-of-factly, as if everything was settled. Tory decided it was foolish to discuss it any further, but she knew very well that a trip to India was about as possible for her as a trip to Mars.

From the supermarket they went to the five-and-ten, which evoked as many exclamations from Santha as the supermarket. "Santha spends all her money in the tencent store," Ravi said. "But why is it called a five-and-ten?" he asked. "There are things in this store that cost many dollars."

"I know. When they first started out, I guess everything was a nickel or a dime, but inflation's changed that. Now everything is expensive."

Santha couldn't resist so many tempting things to buy, and by the time they left she had a bag filled with miniature cosmetics and another bag of pencils, rubber bands, paper clips, and a magnetic can opener, which fascinated her completely.

The Lions Club was giving a luncheon for the young foreign guests, and after walking around the town for a while and after Tory stopped home to change her shorts for a skirt, she took Santha and Ravi over to the town hall, where the luncheon was being held. The building was an old, dilapidated frame structure, badly in need of a coat of paint, and Tory suddenly felt ashamed of it. Her guests didn't say anything, but she saw their look of surprise when she told them it was the town hall. It was the first time in Tory's life she had ever felt a twinge of civic shame.

She had heard her mother complain about the looks of the town hall, and, as a matter of fact, Mrs. Darling had tried to get some of the town leaders to do something about it. Tory remembered, guiltily, that she had criticized her mother for making such a fuss. "What difference does it make what it looks like," Tory had said, "as long as whatever needs to get done in it, gets done? It would be foolish for the town to spend money to fix that old building up—there are probably poor people who need the money more!"

"One has nothing to do with the other," Mrs. Darling had explained patiently. "Money to make the town hall look respectable wouldn't take anything away from poor families. We should be proud of what our town looks like, and the town hall represents the town."

The luncheon was as dull as Tory had expected, and somewhere toward the end of it she started getting butterflies in her stomach. In the excitement of having Santha and Ravi with her, she had been able to push to the back of her mind all her worries about the first day of the canteen.

But now she felt as though she was going to be on exhibit for the whole town to see, since she was the one most people would hold responsible for the outcome of the canteen. Panicked, she looked at the rows of familiar faces at the long lunch tables. In a few hours all these people, both the young crowd and the adults, would come streaming through the wide, red doors of the canteen, each with a critical eye. They would whisper among themselves and examine and point and discuss! She would not be able to explain to them that there was nothing to be done about the slope in the floor, since that was the way the building was, or give any reasons for the other one hundred and one imperfections.

And then an even worse thought occurred to her: supposing no one came. Supposing she and the others waited there all afternoon and no one showed up.

"It can't be that bad." Ravi spoke softly into her ear.

Tory was startled. "What can't be?"

"Whatever you're thinking about. You look worried."

"That's awful! I didn't think it showed!" Tory laughed. "I feel so strongly about most things. I wish I could be more neutral. I either hate something or love it. I rarely feel in-between."

Tory found that she could talk to Ravi easily, as if she had known him for a long time. She was flattered by his interest and attention and impressed with his worldly sophistication. Not only was he older and more traveled, he made her feel like a woman instead of a young girl.

"If you feel strong, you should act strong. One must go with the other," Ravi said.

Tory looked at him in surprise. "I never thought of that. It's an idea . . . if you feel strong, act strong," she repeated. "That *is* an idea."

The conversation made her think of Adam. She had looked around the room when they first came in to see if he was there. He wasn't. And now she looked again, thinking maybe she had missed him, but he was nowhere in sight. Should I act strong with Adam? she wondered. She glanced sideways at Ravi. If he loved a girl, he would go after her; of that Tory was sure. But what was strength in a boy might be aggressiveness in a girl. Besides, there was nothing she could do about Adam. She was sure that no move she could possibly make would change anything between them.

After lunch, while the guests were being shown a group of films, Tory slipped away. She went directly to Amy's house to pick her up on the way to the canteen. While she was waiting for her to get ready, Tory sat down on the back porch. She could see Mrs. Honeycomb's carriage house, and she thought about the day in June when she and Amy first had the idea for the canteen. It seemed like a million years ago, and yet when Tory thought of all that had been accomplished in those few short months, she felt a surge of pride. And I was the one who caused it to happen! she thought. Beneath her pride she felt uneasy, because she heard a mocking voice whisper, "You are just like your mother!" Perhaps she really was fighting with herself when she fought with her mother.

Amy came out and interrupted her thoughts. "Come on, let's go." Amy took her arm.

"I'm nervous, aren't you?" Tory asked.

"Certainly not," Amy said briskly. "We did a fabulous job, and if they don't like it, they're crazy."

Tory laughed. "You're right. But I wish my stomach would understand it."

The girls hurried their steps as they approached the canteen. Much to their surprise there were several large boxes of flowers and a plant waiting outside the door.

"Oh, we have some presents," Tory cried with delight. There was a box of flowers from the Chamber of Commerce, one from the Lions Club, and one from the P.T.A. The beautiful plant was from Tory's parents. Tory's throat felt tight as she read the card in her mother's handwriting: "Welcome and good luck to the canteen; we are all proud of what our young people have done, and we are especially proud to be Tory's Mom and Dad." She had to turn her face away and brush some tears aside, before she could carry the plant inside.

Amy and Tory arranged the flowers and put the plant in a place of honor in the entrance. Then they alternated between admiring the canteen and worrying about what everyone else would think of it. Soon the others who had worked on it came along, then a few guests arrived, and then suddenly the place was jammed with people.

Tory couldn't believe it was true. She was busy being a hostess, taking her turn at pouring punch or tea. Whenever she looked around and caught Amy's eye, the two girls smiled at each other unbelievingly.

"It's a success," Amy whispered to her once as she hurried by. "They're all mad about it."

"They seem to be, don't they?" Tory said in wonder. "Amy, we did it — all of us, and without their help. Isn't it wonderful?"

"Mrs. Honeycomb is positively ecstatic," Amy said, picking up a tray of sandwiches to pass around.

Tory felt choked up with emotion. She was proud of the canteen, and today the trials and tribulations of the summer seemed a joke. But she still had the same nagging feeling of emptiness that had been plaguing her for so many months. So now there was a canteen in Squash Hollow. Would that really make a great difference in her life?

Tomorrow Ravi and Santha would be gone. Although they had been visitors for such a short time, she knew she would sorely miss them. And Adam was still far away. Would he ever be more than someone whom she dreamed about?

As for her mother, Tory had truly wanted to show her appreciation of the plant. She went over to thank her and heard her saying what a pity it was that the floor sloped! Tory found herself stiffly saying "thank you," and turning away. Adam was watching her, and she flushed uncomfortably. Leave it to her mother to find something to criticize, Tory thought unhappily.

Chapter 8

IT WAS toward the end of the afternoon and the canteen was thinning out, when Tory noticed Adam hovering about and sensed that he wanted to talk to her. The afternoon had been a huge success. It seemed to Tory that everyone in Squash Hollow had appeared, and their comments had all been most favorable.

Now she and Amy and the rest of the committee were exhausted. Tory felt like an automaton, walking around politely talking to people with a frozen smile on her face. She caught Adam's eye, and he walked over to her.

"How about coming and sitting down for a minute?" Adam suggested, taking her by the arm.

"Nothing I'd love better," Tory said wearily. "What a day this has been!"

Adam led her over to a bench against the wall in a

quiet corner, and they both sat down. "You've done quite a job here," Adam said. "It's fabulous."

"We all did it. You did your share," Tory said.

"But none of it would have happened if it hadn't been for you. You were the guiding light, shall we say?"

"I don't think so," Tory said. "I don't cherish being a guiding light. Sounds too pious for me."

"I only meant it as a compliment," Adam said. He stared moodily down at his hands. "Don't be so suspicious! The trouble with you is that you're fighting with yourself all the time. Some people are born leaders and some are followers. You're a leader, so why don't you accept it gracefully? After all, you come by it honestly from your mother."

"Maybe two leaders are too many in one family." Tory spoke in a tired voice. Now Adam, too. He probably worshiped Mrs. Darling, and would like Tory to be like her.

"Maybe," Adam said, noncommittally. "But it ain't necessarily so. You're different from your mother, too. Much stronger, I think."

"Is this your polite way of calling me aggressive?" Tory asked. Even in her weariness, a spark of resentment flared up.

"I didn't use the word, you did."

"When a male calls a female strong, he usually has that other hideous word in the back of his mind. Well, to tell you the truth I don't know what I am. I wish I did. I must say I feel anything but strong. Santha has got me thinking. She knows what she is and where she stands. The ground rules are all clear for her. She knows what everyone expects of her. Here everything is mixed up and we make up our own rules as we go along. I don't know how anyone survives!"

Tory stared defiantly at Adam after her outburst. She hadn't meant to say so much, but she couldn't bear to have Adam, of all people, lecturing her. Not now, not today, when she was so tired and nervous, and especially when she had hoped he was approaching her with some idea of patching up their problems, of getting them back on their old footing. What a fool she was to think she had read affection in his eyes!

"I think you're making a lot out of nothing," Adam said coolly. "All this talk about everything being confused; maybe you're doing the confusing."

"That's easy for you to say." Tory tried to keep her voice under control. "It's much easier for a boy than for a girl, and for a man than for a woman."

"Then you ought to be a little more sympathetic to your mother," Adam said calmly. "Did it ever occur to you that she might have problems, too? She lives in the same country you do, not in India."

Tory stared at Adam in wonder. "I never thought of that," she said. "You surprise me, Adam. You act as if you don't see anything at all, and you notice everything. It's scary."

"Beware. I'm the seeing eye. I see all of the universe," Adam said in a low, melodramatic voice. And then he laughed. "I'm a very smart fella. I wish you'd recognize that."

"But I do. I do indeed." Tory felt that the air might be clearing. "I often think about how smart you are."

"You mean you do think about me sometimes?" Adam looked at her quizzically.

"Yes, I do," Tory said, looking straight at him. His eyes held hers until she had to turn away.

"I think of you too," he said. "A great deal." He sat facing her, as if there was more that he wanted to say. Finally he murmured, "Maybe someday we'll understand each other," and he stood up.

"I hope so," Tory said softly. She felt as if there was much more to say, but slowly they walked back to the kitchen to join the others in cleaning up.

Ravi greeted Tory as if she had been away for hours, saying he had been looking all over for her. She saw Adam glance at him and then at her, and she wished she had the courage to tell him that while she liked Ravi enormously, he meant nothing more to her than a friend.

That evening the play went off better than Tory had

expected, and the dance that followed was a gala affair. Tory was flattered, but also a bit embarrassed by Ravi's constant attention. He hardly left her side for a moment, and seemed to think it proper for her to give him all her dances. When someone cut in on him he gave her up gracefully, but then thought it was a great joke to cut right back. Tory was disappointed that Adam didn't cut in on her once. She noticed that he wasn't dancing very much himself, and that he spent most of the evening sitting on the side lines talking. She was relieved that at least he was not giving his attention to anyone in particular. Why did they clash so! In the back of her mind she kept going over the conversation they had had in the afternoon, and she was especially alarmed at one thing he had said in passing—"Don't be so suspicious!" Was she? Was that at the root of her trouble? Didn't she really trust people? Couldn't she accept love, affection, help? The thought was a frightening one, and she pushed it from her mind.

That night, when the two girls were getting ready for bed, Santha told Tory that Ravi was really serious about inviting her to India.

Tory laughed. "He may be serious, but I'd never be able to go. It's too far and too expensive."

"Don't be too sure. You don't know Ravi," Santha said. "When he makes up his mind he usually gets his own way. Indian men are very stubborn. Besides, it would be a good thing for you. I would like you to come to India. You cannot imagine how different it is for girls in my country."

"I know. I was telling Adam a little about it this afternoon. In some ways I think it's easier. In your country a girl has everything arranged for her. She doesn't have to face a lot of problems and make a lot of decisions. Her husband is picked out, she knows she's going to live with her husband's family, she stays home with her babies—her life is very simple and uncomplicated."

"Would you like to have your husband chosen for you?" Santha objected. "Would you like to be a daughter-in-law in his mother's house? Oh, no! A girl has a mind, feelings, ideas, it is all wrong to treat her like a dumb animal. We have to educate our women so that they can think and work and act the way Western women do. We do not want them to stay the way they are!"

"But I wonder if they'll be any happier if you change their ways," Tory mused. "Women here have a lot of freedom I know, but they also have a lot of problems. Sometimes I wish I were living in the Victorian age, when girls stayed home and played duets and wore marvelous feminine clothes. They spoke French and did lovely handwork, and the men adored them."

"In our country the women have to adore their husbands. It is written in all our old books, 'a husband is a woman's god'!" Santha's dark eyes flashed. "Husbands can beat their wives, starve them, and they sit with downcast eyes and never raise a hand to defend themselves."

"I certainly wouldn't like that," Tory said indignantly. "That's awful! But here we go to the other extreme. Too many boys treat a girl like a pal, instead of someone special and romantic. I don't want to be a boy's pal."

"You mean a special boy," Santha said mischievously. "Is there a special boy you like?"

Tory sighed. "Yes, but I don't know how to let him know it. I used to think he liked me, but now every time we start talking I seem to flare up at him when I don't mean to. It's as if . . . as if, I don't know. . . ." Her voice trailed off.

"As if you were afraid to like someone, perhaps?" Santha asked. "I know what that's like. I, too, am afraid of really liking someone. It is because we are afraid of getting hurt, and we don't trust anyone."

Tory looked at Santha in astonishment. "Do *you* feel that way? You seem so, well, trusting and gentle. You don't have all the rough edges that I do."

"It's the way you feel inside that counts," Santha said. "I always think no one is going to like me. My grandmother told me that knowing how to accept love is the most important thing. She is a very wise woman; she says people think they love, but if you cannot accept love, you do not love at all, you love only yourself."

"I suppose that's what's wrong with me." Tory spoke lightly, but inside she had a sinking feeling that her remark might be true.

The girls were tired and they soon stopped talking. Santha fell asleep quickly, but Tory lay awake, listening to Santha's even breathing and wondering if, when she grew up, she would ever find someone to love who would love her back.

The rest of the week end sped by quickly, and in no time it was Sunday evening and Ravi and Santha had to leave. Tory hated to see them go. Never before had she made good friends with anyone so quickly. "Will you come again, please?" she asked them both.

"Of course. We have to work hard now at school, but later if you ask us, we will come. But you will come to India. You wait and see, I will arrange everything," Ravi promised.

"We'll see," Tory said, smiling.

The whole family, Ethan included, took Ravi and Santha to the train, where they were joined by the rest of their group. All the families seemed sad to see their young guests leave, and the station was filled with fond good-bys and waving hands when the train finally pulled out.

It was hard to get back to normal after such a gay week end, but Tory, too, had to get busy with school-work, and in a few weeks' time the week end seemed like a pleasant dream. Except for Adam. Adam's narrow face was a reality that haunted Tory, and she wished desperately that she could find some way to break through the wall that stood between them.

One afternoon, about six weeks after Santha and Ravi's visit, an important-looking letter was waiting for Tory when she came home from school. Wonderingly, she examined it before she opened it. It was a long, somewhat official-looking envelope, but it was addressed in a delicate foreign handwriting. Mrs. Darling was out, but Ethan was at home and as curious as Tory. "Open it," he cried. "Don't stand there staring at it. Don't you want to see what's inside?"

"Of course I do. I was just trying to figure out where it came from."

"Well, for crying out loud! Open it and find out!" Ethan turned away in disgust, but in a second he was back, peering over Tory's shoulder as she read the letter.

It was a letter from Ravi's father, formally inviting Tory and "any friend you would like to choose who would care to visit our country" to spend a holiday in New Delhi in the spring, when Ravi would be home on vacation. "We would like you to stay here in our home as our guests, and we have arranged for your transportation to be at half the rate. That is, you will pay for one way and have round-trip accommodations. We are sorry that it cannot be completely free, but you will have no other expenses whatsoever. It will be a great honor to us to have you here. . . ."

Ethan let out a hoot. "How about that! So you're going to India. Oh boy, some people have all the luck!"

Tory was dumfounded. She stared at the thin piece of writing paper in her hand and read it all over again from the beginning. Ethan kept jumping about wildly, until finally Tory said, "This doesn't mean I'm going. Probably even the half fare costs a fortune. I'd want Amy to come with me, but her mother could never afford it! Oh dear, there's not another soul I'd want to take!"

"Take me," Ethan cried. "I'll go with you."

"You're too young. Besides, Mother and Dad would never let us both go, or pay for us both. They probably won't even let me go!"

"You'll go. I know you. You'll work it somehow."

Tory looked at her younger brother in astonishment, as if she hadn't quite seen him before. "What makes you say a thing like that? Do you think I get everything I want?"

"You make an awfully good stab at it," Ethan said dryly. "Yes, you usually do get what you want—at least, you don't let many things stand in your way."

"I wish that were true," Tory said. "But you make me sound like someone who pushes people around."

"You try," Ethan said, and bounced out of the room.

Tory was upset by Ethan's words. Out of the mouths of babes, she thought unhappily. How could someone feel unsure and scared inside, and still give the impression that she was strong enough to push people around and get what she wanted? It seemed unbelievable to her. And the one thing she really wanted, which was Adam, was farther from her now than ever.

But her thoughts quickly came back to the letter she held in her hand. New Delhi, India—she had a vision of veiled women, walled gardens, strange, spicy smells, crowded bazaars, and tall, handsome men wearing white homespun clothes like those Ravi had. What an opportunity! She might never have a chance like this again. She had to go. She simply had to. This was one time when she was determined not to let anything or anyone stand in her way.

But what about Amy? She had to think of some way for her to go with her. Her mind was in a whirl of excitement. An invitation to visit India! Wait till her mother saw this!

Chapter 9

WHEN Mrs. Darling came home, Tory was still in a daze of excitement. She handed her mother the letter and watched her face as she read it. Mrs. Darling turned to Tory with a laugh. "That's very nice. It's too bad India isn't nearer. How was school today? Do you have a lot of homework? Where's Ethan? I want him to get a haircut."

"Mother, did you read that letter?" Tory asked in a dry voice.

"Certainly I read it. You watched me. I said I think it's very nice. You'll have to answer it."

"Of course I'll answer it!" Tory said impatiently. "But did you read what it says? Ravi's father wants me to come to New Delhi. Isn't that the most wonderful thing you ever heard?" Tory's eyes shone with excitement.

143

Her mother gave her a startled glance. "It's very nice of him to ask you. Indian people have a reputation for being extremely hospitable, and I'm sure they would like you to come. But I also suspect he knows it is very unlikely that you can. Now I must get Ethan to the barber before it's too late."

"But Mother, why can't I go?"

Mrs. Darling stopped on her way out and looked at her daughter in astonishment. "Now Tory, don't tell me you take this invitation seriously? It's just a polite way for Ravi's father to thank us for having Ravi and Santha here. It's perfectly ridiculous for you to think for a moment of going to India. New Delhi, for heaven's sake! It's too far away and too expensive. I wouldn't dream of letting you travel that distance alone."

"But I would be going with Ravi, and he says to bring a friend. I've been thinking about Amy, of course —if only there was some way to get the money for her."

"Tory, stop living in a dream world. It's preposterous for you to daydream about going to India and to think of getting Amy involved. The whole idea is absurd. I really must find Ethan now." Mrs. Darling hurried out of the house to the back yard, calling Ethan as she went.

When Tory heard the car pull out of the driveway, she immediately ran to the telephone to call Amy and tell her the news. "My mother doesn't take it seriously," she ended up. "She says the whole idea is ridiculous. But you know, Amy, I don't think so. If Ravi and Santha and thousands of other foreign students manage to get over here, I don't see why you and I can't go to New Delhi. Do you think that's crazy?" She stopped for breath.

Amy's voice was slow in answering. "I don't think it's crazy—I think it's impossible. I can't think the way you do, Tory. You know, the way you were about the canteen. You looked out back and saw Mrs. Honeycomb's carriage house, and in two minutes flat you had the idea for the canteen, and the next minute we were over there asking her about it. I think you're terrific, but it's not the way I am. Now you get a letter inviting you to India, and boom, you're going to find a way to go."

"Well, I can't think of anything in two minutes this time," Tory said with a laugh. "But you're right. I am going to find a way to go, and take you with me, too. Would you go?"

"I don't see how I could. I can't leave my mother and the kids, and besides, we'd never have the money for the fare. It's impossible."

"Nothing is impossible," Tory said firmly. "You wait and see, I'll figure out something."

"You probably will," Amy agreed. "I don't know how or what, but I'm sure you will."

When Tory hung up the phone she went upstairs to her room, her mind going around and around. But as she looked at her room her confidence left her. Everyone said she could figure out a way to do anything, but she still hadn't figured out how to do her room the way she wanted. It was in exactly the same state that it had been in all summer. Her shorn four-poster bed looked naked without its canopy and skirt, and the rest of the room had the same little bows and doodads in it. Tory knew perfectly well that all she had to do was ask her mother to help her fix it up, and it would get done, but she was determined not to do that. She and her mother were each playing a waiting game. Every once in a while Mrs. Darling would say, "We must do something about your room." She might add, "There's a sale on drapery fabrics downtown. Do you want to see what there is?" And Tory would shake her head and say, "No, thank you." Her mother did not pursue the subject, but they both knew that Mrs. Darling felt Tory should accept her help while Tory felt exactly the opposite. They had reached a deadlock—like the cold war, it might go on for years.

Tory sighed unhappily. How could she possibly get to New Delhi, when she didn't even have the strength of character to get permission to redecorate her own room in her own way? Life was very discouraging.

Tory sat disconsolately on her bed, thinking. Since

the Chamber of Commerce had invited Ravi and Santha to Squash Hollow, they might conceivably want to send two young Americans to India for a return visit. But Tory rejected that idea promptly. She didn't want to get mixed up with any of her mother's organizations. Then the obvious idea hit her. Why not have the canteen do it?

Tory sat up straight, and her face broke into a smile. It was a perfect idea. The more she thought about it, the better she liked it. It could be a real international cultural exchange. It would be a great thing for the canteen and the town. Tory saw herself and Amy as two emissaries bringing greetings to India from an old New England town in the United States, and telling the young people in New Delhi how a great democracy works. They would bring home to their classmates and friends a wealth of information on the customs and ideas of an Oriental land many thousands of miles away.

Tory went on daydreaming and enjoying herself enormously. The one thing she was vague about was how to convince her mother to let her go, but she was sure she would be able to do that.

Tory did not say a word to her mother about the trip when she came home with Ethan from the barber's. She decided she would wait until the family was together at the dinner table before she broached the subject and her plan.

As it turned out, Tory wasn't the one to bring up the subject, because as soon as they sat down to eat, Ethan asked Mr. Darling if he knew that Tory had been invited to visit India. "No, I don't know a thing about it," Mr. Darling said.

Tory ran to get the letter and showed it to her father. He had an amused smile on his face as he read it. "This is a beautiful letter, and something for you to save," he said.

"Oh, I wouldn't throw it away for the world! But Daddy, don't you think I ought to go?" Tory demanded.

Mr. Darling was startled. "It doesn't seem very practical," he said dryly. "Even half fare is a lot of money, and you'll have plenty of time to travel when you're older."

"But you and Mother think it's marvelous for all these young people to come here from other countries," Tory exclaimed. "Santha's only a year older than I am."

"Yes, how about that?" Ethan chimed in.

"Those youngsters come here to be educated. Their countries need American skills and know-how. They're not just coming here for the fun of it," Mr. Darling said.

"But don't you think Americans should know something about other countries?" Tory demanded. "We can't live like ostriches with our heads in the sand."

"This is all quite beside the point," Mrs. Darling said, looking from one to the other, and then letting her eyes rest on Tory. "The fact is that I wouldn't dream of letting you go to India. You are much too young and it's too far away. If we were all going it would be different, although I would never want to travel that far. But for you to go alone, without an adult, would be out of the question, Tory. I think it's silly for you to take this letter seriously, I told you that this afternoon. Let's not have a family quarrel—let's just forget about it."

Tory's eyes flashed. She waited for her mother to finish speaking, and then she burst out indignantly, "Really, Mother, you talk as if I were a little baby, and I must say you contradict yourself terribly! You think it's wonderful for Ravi and Santha to come here, and thousands of other students, but when it comes to letting your precious sixteen-year-old daughter go visit them, then suddenly you object. Don't you think that's a bit hypocritical?"

"Tory, I don't want you talking that way to your mother," Mr. Darling said sharply.

"It's all right," Mrs. Darling said soothingly. "Maybe Tory does have a point and I'm willing to admit it. Yes, I do feel different about my own daughter than I do about Santha and Ravi. Maybe if I were their mother I would want my children to have the benefits of an American education. But I can't bear the thought of sending you off to India. Right or wrong that's the way I feel about it, and I'm afraid you'll just have to accept it, Tory."

"And what if I don't?" Tory asked. "You always manage to find an excuse for what you do. You always put me in the wrong. Well, this time I think I'm right, and I think it's something worth fighting for. Do I have to accept what you think? If the canteen raised the money to send me, I don't see how you could stop me from going." Tory spoke slowly and deliberately and, while her heart was pounding, she managed to sound fairly calm.

"We certainly can stop you," Mr. Darling said angrily, "and I do not like your tone of voice or what you have to say. You may think you are grown-up, but you are still a child."

"I think you're both taking an unreasonable position," Tory cried, deciding, since she had gone this far, she might as well go the whole way. "Especially Mother. She's always talking about one world and international relations, and she wants people to be concerned about important issues. Well, from where I sit, it's all a lot of talk. When it comes to her own daughter, she says she's too young to participate. I won't ever believe what she says from now on. You can scold me all you like, but I have a right to my opinion and you can't change that!" Tory stopped for breath. "And what's more," she added, addressing her mother, "I'm going to see if the canteen will raise the money to send Amy and me, and if they do and you try to stop me, then the whole town will know what a hypocrite you are!" Her ears pounding with the sound of her own voice, Tory got up and hurriedly left the table. She didn't know what might happen next. Never in her life had she spoken to her parents this way, and she was shaking with both fear and a certain satisfaction. She felt as if something that had been festering within her had finally been torn out and exposed.

She ran up to her room, angry, hurt, frightened, and defiant. Breathing hard, she sat down on her bed, feeling as if the house must come down on top of her. She suddenly realized she was starving. If only she had eaten her supper before exploding this way. But it was too late now. Happily she remembered a bar of chocolate in her jacket pocket, bought on her way home from school. She munched on that, feeling somewhat like a refugee.

It seemed hours later that she heard her mother coming up the stairs and then a light knock on her door.

"Come in," Tory said. She was amazed at how calm her mother's face looked, as if nothing unusual had happened.

Mrs. Darling sat down on the chair facing Tory, who was stretched out on her bed. "I do not like the way you spoke to me, or to your father," Mrs. Darling spoke quietly. "But I am willing to admit that I have to give very serious thought to what you said. I pride myself that I can take criticism, and I must consider it seriously when it comes from my own daughter. I don't know if your accusations are right. I do not think I am a hypocrite, because I believe a mother is entitled to be emotional about her daughter. And I don't believe everyone is capable of practicing what he preaches, but that doesn't make what he preaches wrong. Perhaps I am not sophisticated enough to let you do what I think other girls should do—I don't know, I have to think about it."

"I'm sorry that I lost my temper," Tory said.

"I'm glad you said that. But I really came up here to discuss something else with you. If you are serious about asking the canteen to raise money to send you and Amy to India, I want to beg you not to do it. And not for the reasons you think," she added hurriedly as Tory began to object. "This has nothing to do with the way I feel about your going, this is strictly town politics. Tory, can't you see that it would be in the worst possible taste for you to ask the canteen to raise money to send you and Amy to India? Why you and Amy? You would be using an organization of which you are the head for your own personal advantage. I think it would be shocking and would wreck the canteen!"

Tory stared at her mother in surprise. "No one would think of that but you!" she exclaimed. "The point is that I was invited and asked to bring someone. Naturally it will be up to the canteen to decide if they want to do it, but I can't see anything wrong in it. You go to lots of places as a delegate for the organizations you belong to. It's about the same thing."

"I'm afraid not." Mrs. Darling shook her head. "A delegate is elected. If the canteen wants to raise money in order to send two people to India, that's one thing. But how they choose the two people—by elections, drawing lots, or whatever—is something else. You can't ask them to send two people and say one of them must be me and the other my best friend. Really, Tory, no organization can work that way. I've had experience, and I know what I'm talking about."

"I'm going to find out for myself," Tory said stubbornly. "I don't see any harm in it, and I don't think the other kids in the canteen will either. If they do agree with me, will you let me go?" She looked at her mother hopefully.

"I don't know. I just don't know. I'll have to give it a lot of thought." Mrs. Darling stood up.

When her mother left, Tory sat down at her desk and made up a list of the members of the canteen's steering committee. She would call them for a special meeting.

Chapter 10

TORY was able to get everyone together two nights later. She felt at home with the steering committee, which was comprised of the same group that had first met to get the canteen started. She was convinced that they would be as enthusiastic as she about her invitation to visit India. After thinking it over carefully, Tory had decided not to discuss her ideas with Amy. Amy was timid and conservative, and would be sure to find objections. It would be better to let her hear about it with the others.

Tory dressed carefully for the meeting. She wanted to make the best impression possible. As a matter of fact, she felt proud of the calm, mature way she was handling the whole problem. She had not discussed it any further with her mother, merely saying she would take it up at a meeting with the others, but inwardly

155

she was in a turmoil. All she could think of was the trip. The day after the letter arrived she spent the afternoon at the library looking at all their books on India, and she came home with five of them hidden in her brief case. At night she dreamed of temples, swamis, and bazaars; of beautiful women plaiting their hair, bracelets jangling on their arms, their bodies smelling of incense and draped in silk-brocaded saris; and of tall, dark men in beautiful white coats and jodhpurs. It was a world that fascinated her with its mystery. She was sure it was fate that had sent Ravi and Santha to her house and that going to India was part of her destiny.

The meeting was at Amy's house, and Tory deliberately arrived just in time to start the meeting, and consequently had no opportunity to tell anyone what it was about. Everyone was waiting for her, and she wasted no time getting started.

The first thing she did was to read the letter. There was excitement in her voice, and her heart was beating nervously until she finished. There was a moment's silence, and then Helen Fisher said, "That's very nice, but what has it got to do with us, with the canteen?"

This was not the reaction Tory had anticipated. She had somehow expected an enthusiastic reflection of her own excitement, but looking around at the faces of the others she saw that, with the exception of Amy and Adam, they weren't very interested in her invitation to visit India.

Her heart sank, but while she was fumbling for the right words to say, Amy came to her rescue. "It has to do with all of us," Amy explained, "because Santha and Ravi came here partly as guests of the canteen. And it should mean something to all of us that our chairman has been invited back to their country. I think we should do something about it."

Tory felt self-conscious as the group looked at her.

"What is there for *us* to do?" Gary Sutton asked.

"Yes, what *are* we supposed to do?" someone said.

They looked from Amy to Tory questioningly. Tory's mind went blank, and all her ideas fled completely. Her mother's warning hammered in her head.

"Well, there are practical problems about going to India," Adam said in his slow drawl. "Things like money, you know."

"Yes." Amy picked up the cue from Adam. "I think it would be great if the canteen raised the money to send Tory to visit Ravi's family in New Delhi. It would be a marvelous thing to do."

"Yes, and how about sending me to Paris?" one of the twins said.

"That's what I say," Helen Fisher said in a loud,

clear voice. "Why should we raise money to send Tory to India? What good is that going to do the rest of us or the canteen?"

"That's a good question," the Sutton boys chorused. "What good *is* it going to do us? What have you got to say, Tory?"

Tory cleared her throat nervously. "Well, I thought it would mean something to the canteen," she said lamely. "I thought it was an honor for all of us, and while I'm the one who is invited, it really is a reflection on the whole group. If I go, and someone—Amy, for instance, comes with me, we will be going as representatives of the canteen, and it will mean a great deal. Like having Santha and Ravi and the others here. I think we all got a lot out of their visit, even just for the week end. A return trip would be sort of a cultural exchange between our two countries." Her voice had gotten stronger as she spoke, but now it trailed off uncertainly.

"I think it would be great," Adam said emphatically. "After all, Tory got this canteen started, and if we can raise the money to send her to India, it will be a wonderful achievement for all of us. Tory should go as our chairman, and we should choose one other person to go with her. I don't care if it's Amy—that's fine with me."

"Sounds fine," Eileen said.

Several of the group nodded approval. But Helen Fisher sprang to her feet. "I think this is the most undemocratic thing I ever heard of. We're not a charitable organization, or a travel agency, raising money to send a couple of kids off on a vacation. I never heard of such a thing—it makes me sick! I'm going to resign." She sat down with a thump.

"Well, you don't have to get so excited," Adam said calmly. "And no one's sending anybody off on a vacation, although that's not such a bad idea either. But what do you suggest?"

Helen sat perched like a bird with ruffled feathers. "Well, I think we have to go into this whole thing very thoroughly and examine it carefully. If we do decide it's a good idea to raise money to send two representatives to India, and with such a marvelous invitation we should, then they should be elected, or chosen by the whole canteen. I don't think they should be decided on beforehand. It just isn't fair!"

"Why couldn't we draw lots?" Eileen asked. "Then everyone will have a chance. It will be something like a raffle. Everyone in the canteen would be willing to work for it, because he'd have a chance to win. I think that would be wonderful."

"That's a good idea," the Sutton boys said, and the twins added their approval.

"What do you think?" Amy turned to Tory.

Tory was exhausted from the strain of trying to conceal all her emotions. She felt limp and soggy, as if she had been walking in the rain all night. "I don't think it's up to me to say," Tory spoke in a low voice. "I don't want to do anything that's undemocratic. If you think it's better to choose, that's all right with me."

"I think it's a dirty trick," Adam said. "Tory's the one who got the invitation, and it makes the trip financially possible. She's our chairman. Why shouldn't she go? How do we know they want someone else?" he demanded.

"I think if Tory wants to go, she has to go on her own," Helen Fisher said. "If she wants to make it a matter for the canteen, then she has to write to Mr. What's-his-name, Ravi's father, and explain that she would like to turn the invitation over to us. If that is all right with him, then we will choose two members to go as our representatives by drawing lots."

"I'd like to see Tory go, you all know that, but I think Helen is right." Amy spoke slowly, with her eyes on Tory's face. "Let's vote on it," she suggested, reluctantly.

"Is everyone ready to vote," Tory asked, looking around the group unhappily, but trying to be very businesslike. "Did you make a motion, Amy?"

"Let Helen make it, it was her idea," Amy said.

Helen made the motion, repeating what she had said. The motion was approved by everyone except Adam, who didn't vote at all.

The meeting broke up quickly, and Tory rushed to leave. Amy ran over to her before she went out the door. "I hope you're not angry with me. But I had to do what I thought was right. I know when you think about it, you'll agree, too."

"I'm not angry. Don't be silly. But I have to run now." Tory hurried away, wanting to be alone. She didn't even want Amy with her. She loved her dearly, but right now her forthrightness and sympathy were more than Tory could bear.

Out on the street she heard steps coming after her and then Adam's voice calling softly. "Hey, Tory, what's your hurry?"

Tory whirled around. "You startled me. I'm just going home."

"Mind if I walk with you?"

Tory shook her head. "No, I guess not," she said, realizing she didn't sound very cordial.

"Well, I'm going to walk with you whether you like it or not." Adam fell into step beside her. "I was sorry about tonight. It looked as if everyone was ganging up on you, but I don't think that's what they meant."

"I don't care," Tory said. "If I really want to go to India, I guess my folks will pay for it." She didn't mean what she was saying. Her words sounded as false to her as they must to Adam, and she was ashamed of how foolish and childish she must seem. But she was too upset to let go the least little bit. Any second she might burst into tears. She wanted to be home and alone in her own room.

"I thought you might want to know why I didn't vote along with the rest," Adam said shortly.

"I thought because you probably didn't agree with them," Tory said, helpless in her own defensiveness and wishing she didn't sound so cold to Adam.

"Well, partly I didn't agree with them, but I guess I always side with the minority. Besides, I think you deserve to go."

"But you're the one who thinks I'm too pushy and aggressive. I'd have thought you'd be the first to say I was just trying to get the canteen to finance a trip for me!"

"That's a mean thing to say!" Adam cried. "I might have thought so, except I think I know you better. Maybe I'm wrong. To tell you the truth, I sided with you because everyone was against you, even Amy. I thought you needed help."

"That's very big of you indeed! What are you trying to tell me? That you really agreed with the others, but out of the goodness of your soul, you came to my rescue. Thanks a lot!"

"And if I did that, what's wrong with it?" Adam demanded angrily. "Do you think you're above needing help? That's your whole trouble. You can't accept anything from anyone. You don't know how to accept friendship, affection, probably not even love. I don't think you've ever loved anyone in your whole life, and that's why you don't understand how people feel when they love you. I don't think you love your own mother! Oh yes, you probably say you love her, but have you ever stopped to think what it means? It means wanting to do things for the person you love, but you resent it any time your mother wants to do something for you or anybody else. Don't think I didn't know you hated it when she asked me over for all those dinners. You couldn't stand her doing something for me. And you had to treat me like dirt, the poor little waif your mother was taking in. You couldn't even go to the dance with me. You hated her and you had to hate me too!"

They had both slowed up while Adam talked, and now they stood in front of Tory's house, facing each other. Tory stared at Adam incredulously. She couldn't say a word, because her throat was tight with sobs. "Oh, Adam," she finally said. "It wasn't like that at all—how can people misunderstand each other so!" The tears rolled down her cheeks. "I thought you were just being polite, that you asked me to the dance because you felt you had to, and I couldn't stand that. I can't stand to have anyone feel sorry for me." She was going to burst into tears in a minute, so she mumbled good night and then fled into the house and straight up to her room.

With the door safely closed behind her, she flung herself down on the bed and let the sobs come. For Adam to talk this way to her—it was too much. She couldn't bear to think of anything now—of the canteen or the trip to India. With the sobs still shaking her, she tore off her clothes and crawled underneath the covers. She wanted to stay there forever and never have to see Adam, the canteen, even Amy, again.

Chapter 11

THE next morning, when Tory woke up, the sun was streaming into her room. She opened her eyes and then closed them again, not wanting to face the day. At first she didn't remember why; then memory came flooding back. She turned her face against the pillow, longing to stay that way. Soon, however, the warm sun, the smell of coffee coming up from the kitchen, and the realization that today was Saturday and there was no school, impelled her to get up out of bed.

Her mood was a peculiar one. She was worn out from last night's emotional stress and all her weeping, and she felt empty. She also felt as if something new was about to happen to her. It was nothing she could put her finger on, or explain rationally; it was as if her body was molting its old skin and preparing for a brand new state of being. It was an odd sensation and it gave her a tremulous sense of excitement about everything she did. The mere act of getting dressed, of feeling the touch of cotton and nylon against her body and the familiar curve of her sneakers around her feet, of stroking a brush through her hair—all these seemed to be acts she had done in the past, but would never do again in quite the same way.

With this feeling still accompanying her, Tory went downstairs to breakfast. Ethan and her father had already eaten and gone out, and Mrs. Darling was alone in the kitchen. Her mother said good morning to her and casually asked how last night's meeting had gone.

Before Tory replied she realized that she had been anticipating this moment of crisis. She drank down the glass of orange juice in her hand before answering. "The meeting went terribly," she said, when she had finished, surprised at the calmness of her voice. "You were absolutely right. They thought it was awful of me to ask the canteen to send me to India. I was very thoroughly put in my place by them all, Amy and Adam included."

Her mother turned to her with anxious eyes. "I'm sorry if you had a rough time of it. What did they decide to do?"

"Aren't you even going to say I told you so?" Tory asked. "You warned me, and you were right."

"I was only trying to help you," Mrs. Darling said.

At the word *help*, Tory's assumed, momentary calm left her, and her eyes flooded with tears. "Adam says I don't know how to accept any help," she sobbed suddenly, taking her mother completely by surprise. "He says I'll never love anyone, because I don't know how to let anyone love me. He made me sound like such a monster—and I don't want to be that way. I do want to do things my own way, I know that, but is that such a crime?"

Mrs. Darling held Tory to her, stroking her hair gently. "I'm afraid it's all part of growing up," she said soothingly. "And perhaps Adam was a little hard on you. I'm afraid you rather hurt him last summer, because you couldn't accept his being here so much and you resented my helping him."

"It wasn't your helping him, it was your interfering that bothered me," Tory said drying her eyes. "I felt you were doing something *against* me, not *for* him."

"Me interfere? How can you say such a thing?" Mrs. Darling said in a surprised voice. "Tory, that's the last thing I'd do. My asking Adam here had nothing to do with you."

Tory sighed. "It didn't directly, Mom, I know that." She straightened up out of her mother's arms. The truth was, there were some things her mother would never understand. Tory looked at her with clearer eyes: she is my mother, Tory thought, and she loves me, but that doesn't make her a super woman, who understands everything and does everything the way I'd like her to. This was an important revelation for Tory, and it made her look at her mother with new sympathy and a sense of equality.

"I want to help you, the same way I wanted to help Adam," Mrs. Darling continued. "You don't make it easy—you have a strong will of your own that I don't want to break, but I cannot just sit by and watch you do things that are wrong. I would be a poor mother if I did that, wouldn't I?"

"But doesn't everyone have to learn from his own experience?" Tory asked.

"Within limits. I can't keep you from getting hurt, but I can't help trying to protect you. I suppose that's when you and I run into head-on collisions. If you would only accept the fact that I'm offering help out of love, maybe you wouldn't fight me every inch of the way." Mrs. Darling sighed.

"You mean things like my room?" Tory asked. "I should let you help me do it?"

"I think we could do it together," Mrs. Darling said. "To put it quite simply, your father and I will be paying for any redecoration. You are still under our guidance. After all, it isn't the last room you'll be doing, it's the first. Someday you will have your own home, and this experience will be helpful. Think of this time of your life as a transition between being a child dependent on your parents and being an independent grownup. You're halfway between the two, and that's what makes it hard."

"I think I see what you mean," Tory said thoughtfully. "I never thought of it that way before. I *am* impatient to be grown-up. And I feel so often that I know as much now as I'll ever know, that there's nothing more for me to learn."

Mrs. Darling smiled. "We all feel that way at times, and then we get surprised at how little we do know. You are so absolute, Tory."

You are too, Tory thought to herself. I guess we *are* alike, she reflected, which makes it hard to get along, but she felt that now they were coming to a better understanding.

"We haven't talked like this for a long time, have we?" Tory said, mixing up a pan of scrambled eggs.

"No, I'm afraid not. I'm glad we can, even once in a while. It makes living together easier."

The telephone rang, and Mrs. Darling hurried into the hall to answer it. Tory listened thoughtfully to her mother's voice. It still irritated her; she wished her mother didn't speak on the phone in that oversweet way. But that's her problem, she thought, not mine. Deliberately she closed her ears to her mother's voice and was amazed at how easy it was to do.

When her mother came back to the kitchen, Tory told her what the committee had decided to do. "Now I have to write a letter to Ravi's father," she ended up. "Unless you and Daddy would like to send me to India," she added.

"I'm afraid we can't afford it," Mrs. Darling said.

"Would you let me go if I won?" Tory asked.

"I don't suppose we could stop you," her mother said. "I wouldn't like it, but I guess I'd have to let you go. I have to let you grow up; there are some things you're going to do that I may not like for my own reasons; but if they aren't *wrong* things I'll have to go along with them. And it works both ways, Tory. You have to accept the things I do that you don't like—I was probably doing them before you were born, and I can't stop now."

"What about my room?" Tory asked.

"What about it? What do you want to do?"

"Well, I thought since the bedposts are cut, I'd like to get rid of the frame altogether. Just put the box spring and mattress on legs and make a studio bed out of it."

Mrs. Darling shrugged. "Well, I guess that's the only thing left that you can do with it."

"And I'd like to do the whole room in black and white. I think that would be stunning, don't you?"

Mrs. Darling narrowed her eyes as if she were trying

to visualize it. "I think that would be too stark. You should have some color in it. What about black, gold, and red? You could have a gold-covered bedspread and put black and red cushions on it. A red rug would be bright and pretty, and then we can see about the drapes. Perhaps a stripe would be nice, with lots of different colors."

"That sounds like a terrible hodgepodge. I want it stark and dramatic. I want to keep it all black and white. A black bedspread with white pillows, and a big white fluffy rug, and I suppose white curtains, and I could paint my chest black. . . ."

"Tory, you cannot paint that chest. You will ruin it. That beautiful walnut, we paid a fortune for it. Once you paint it, it will become a cheap, ordinary piece." Mrs. Darling's eyes were shocked and troubled.

"Well, here we go again." Tory sighed. "We're right back where we started from with the bed, Mom. It's my chest, isn't it? Do we have to go through all that again?"

"There's no need for you to be rude." Mrs. Darling looked more hurt than ever.

"I'm not being rude! This is what drives me crazy. You make all these fine speeches, and you sound so sympathetic and understanding, and then the minute I want to do something my way instead of yours, it's the end. Then you're just like any other old-fashioned mother!"

"I could say the same to you, Tory. You sound very mature when you talk, and then you act like a little spoiled baby when you want to do something destructive, and I say no. And I do say no to painting that chest. This is exactly what I've been talking about. I cannot permit you to do any foolish thing that comes into your head."

"I guess we'll never get along!" Tory burst out.

"I didn't expect it would be smooth," Mrs. Darling said. "We're going to have disagreements, Tory, and you are going to have to continue to obey your father and me at times when you may not agree with us or even fully understand why—but that's the way it is until you grow up."

"And I'll just continue to shout my disagreements, that's all."

"I dare say we'll all live through it. But you don't have to make such terrible faces, Tory! It's really not the end of the world, because you can't paint that chest. You can do the colors the way you want, pick out the fabrics within a reasonable price, and use your own taste for all of it. But you cannot spoil good furniture. That's fair, isn't it?"

"I suppose so," Tory agreed grudgingly. Then she felt sorry and realized she was acting in a childish manner. "I'm sorry, Mom," she said, giving her a kiss with genuine affection.

Tory wondered if anything was ever going to be splendid and marvelous again, or even totally terrible. Was it always going to be compromise, compromise—getting only half of what she wanted, and having to give up the other half?

"Can we go shopping for a bedspread and curtains today?" she asked her mother, thinking she had better take her mother's offer as quickly as possible before she changed her mind.

"Yes, of course we can. As soon as we get the house straightened up."

Tory went up to her room lost in thought. She felt older and wiser, as if life, with all its endless contradictions, was unfolding before her.

Chapter 12

TORY spent hours composing her letter to Ravi's father. She wanted to word it just right—expressing her gratitude for his invitation, tactfully suggesting what the canteen would like to do, and nowhere in the letter intimating that she couldn't come because she couldn't afford it. She did not want Mr. Srivastava to think his invitation was in any way wanting. Tory tore up one letter after another, until she finally had a draft that satisfied her. She read it to her mother, and, with a few small corrections, Mrs. Darling agreed that it was good.

When Tory made the final copy and put the letter in the mailbox, she felt as if she were putting the last period to her childhood. A year ago, she reflected, or even at the beginning of the summer, she would have stormed and raged before giving up such an invitation. And it was even harder to turn it over to the canteen so that two other people could go. When Amy pointed out that Tory had just as good a chance of going as anyone else, Tory shook her head and said she was sure she wouldn't win the drawing.

They all waited anxiously for Mr. Srivastava's reply. Tory, however, was more preoccupied with what to do about Adam than anything else. Things had been very strained between them since the night of the meeting. Then Adam's father died, and Tory was at such a loss when she tried to say the right thing to him that she ended up by writing a stiff little note, which she hated.

They spoke to each other in school, but Tory wanted desperately to be alone with him and didn't know how to arrange it. One day, walking home from school, she had a brain storm and ran the rest of the way.

"Mom, Mom." She came into the kitchen breathless. "Would you do me a favor, please?"

"If I can, I'll be glad to," Mrs. Darling promised. "For heaven's sake, sit down and catch your breath."

Tory dumped her books on the kitchen table and sat on the edge of a stool, facing her mother. "It's about Adam. Would you invite him to dinner? I think you should anyway, with his father having died and all. Don't you think it would be nice?"

"Well, this is a new twist," Mrs. Darling said. "I thought you were angry, because I invited him during the summer. Why don't *you* ask him?"

"I can't. I'd rather you did. You're the one who said people change. Well, I'm changing. Aren't you glad?"

"I hope I can keep up with your changes," Mrs. Darling said with a laugh. "Yes, I'll ask Adam to dinner, be glad to. I would have before now, except I thought you'd object. You see, even an old lady like me can change sometimes!"

"You're far from being an old lady," Tory said, grinning. "And I'll have to admit you're very smart," she added, giving her mother a grateful peck on the cheek.

Tory nearly drove herself and her mother crazy worrying about Adam's coming for dinner. "You must have asked me at least a dozen times what we're having to eat," Mrs. Darling complained. "Here's the menu, and I hope it suits you: fried chicken and rice, broccoli, sliced tomatoes, and chocolate layer cake. I know Adam loves every one of these things, so please relax."

"Does he like broccoli? Are you sure? I don't think anyone really likes broccoli, I think they just tolerate it."

"Adam likes it, take my word for it. He always asked for it last summer, when I couldn't get it. Here, you can put the frosting on the cake." Mrs. Darling handed her a bowl filled with rich, dark chocolate.

Concentrating as if her life depended on it, Tory

frosted the cake, carefully smoothing out each tiny lump. "Mother, do you think Adam will think I'm pushy if I suggest that we go for a walk after supper?"

Mrs. Darling glanced at her daughter in wonder. "No, dear, I don't think so. There's nothing wrong with suggesting a walk."

"I have to be very careful with Adam. He accused me of being aggressive. I wish I were delicate and clingy, like Eileen or Liz Brooks."

"I don't think Adam would like you if you were. He seems to want a girl who has strength of character and personality, but he wants her to make him feel like a male. It counts more from a girl like that than from the kind who clings."

"Do you think so?" Tory asked, finished with the cake and licking the bowl and her fingers. "I hope I can convince him that I think he's the greatest."

"Do you think he is?" her mother asked.

Tory nodded her head, observing her handiwork on the cake with satisfaction. "Yes, I like him a lot. You do too, don't you?" She looked at her mother directly and smiled. "I'm talking too much!"

"No harm done," her mother said casually, but she gave Tory a warm and grateful look.

Tory dressed carefully for the evening. She wanted to look good, but not too dressed-up. She went through her wardrobe slowly and finally decided on a soft, feminine white blouse and a black velveteen skirt that looked all right with low-heeled shoes. She wanted to be able to get Adam out for a walk, and she didn't want to walk with high heels on. While she fixed her hair and put on her make-up she kept glancing out the window to see if Adam had arrived. When he finally did come, she got a real case of stage fright and had to sit in her room for several minutes to regain her composure. "You *are* an idiot," she scolded herself. "It's only Adam, there's nothing to be nervous about!"

Her heart hammered as she went downstairs to greet him, and yet once she said hello to him she wondered why she had been in such a state. It *was* only Adam, and when they all sat down at the dinner table and he began joking with Ethan and her father, it seemed like old times again. He acted very much at home, and he gave no hint of the fight Tory had had with him.

After dinner Tory helped her mother with the dishes, and then joined Adam in the living room, where he was talking with her father. Feeling a little self-conscious, she asked him if he wanted to go for a walk. "Sure," Adam said, and they went out.

It was a cool, starlit evening, and Tory pulled her scarf tight around her head and turned her coat collar up around her chin. "Are you too cold?" Adam asked, walking alongside her.

"No, I like it."

They walked in silence for a while. Tory wished desperately that she knew how to get started on all the things she wanted to tell Adam, but her mind was a blank. The sharp coldness in the air and Adam beside her made her feel tingly and alive. She was afraid, however, that the continued silence would make Adam think she was stupid and dull.

"There's so much I'd like to say to you," she finally burst out, "but I don't know where to begin."

"Begin at the beginning," Adam said with a smile.

"I guess the beginning goes back to the first of the summer. What you said to me about my mother's asking you to dinner every night was partly true. I didn't like it—but not for the reason you said. I. . . ." She faltered.

"Go ahead. Don't be afraid to say what you want," Adam said.

"I'm not afraid—it's just, well, they're hard things to say. I mean for a girl to say to a boy. I thought that you liked me and I knew that I liked you, and then when Mom asked you to come over, it seemed to me she was interfering and it would spoil everything. And it did too—you'll have to agree to that!"

"Something went haywire. But that's all water under the bridge. Can't we start now, from scratch?"

"I'd like to," Tory said.

Adam tucked Tory's arm through his, and they walked on in silence. Tory wondered if they *could* start from scratch now. She didn't know—after a relationship had been as strained as theirs, could they pick it up and go on as if nothing had happened?

Tory sighed. She didn't feel the wonderful glow she had expected to feel, walking beside Adam in the cool, crisp moonlight. It was nice and comfortable and friendly, but not quite the glorious thing she had been dreaming of. Was this, too, part of growing up?

Was nothing ever to be perfect again?

The letter came back from Mr. Srivastava saying that he hoped that Tory would come anyway, but they would be more than delighted to have two young representatives from Squash Hollow and the canteen visit them in New Delhi.

Tory and the committee immediately started working on plans for a dance to raise money. They held a meeting at which they decided to run a drawing, selecting the two representatives, the night of the dance. All of the canteen's members were eligible for the trip to India. Naturally Ravi and Santha were invited to the dance, as were the other foreign students who had visited Squash Hollow.

The committee worked hard on publicizing the dance, but they were all amazed at their success in selling tickets to it. Everyone in Squash Hollow, young and old alike, seemed to be buying tickets for the Dance for India, as they called it. Then one day, when a good-sized check came to the canteen from the Chamber of Commerce, as a contribution to the Dance for India, Tory became suspicious. "It's wonderful!" she said. But that evening she asked her mother if she'd been raising money for the dance.

Mrs. Darling was busy in the kitchen, and she glanced swiftly at Tory. "As a matter of fact, I have," she said. "Any objections?"

Tory could feel her old irritation rise. There was her mother being efficient and helpful again, and trying to take over. Why couldn't she mind her own business?

But Tory waited for the wave of impatience to die down. She didn't say anything to her mother until she was able to run over all the other answers that came to her mind: she not only wants to help, she *is* helping, the canteen needs all the money and help it can get, you should be grateful for it, not angry!

"Of course, there are no objections," Tory finally said calmly. "It's wonderful. Are you going to try to get the P.T.A. and the Women's Auxiliary to contribute, too?"

Mrs. Darling's eyes met Tory's. "Would you like me to?" she asked.

"I think it would be great," Tory said. She felt an

unexpected glow within her as she went out of the
kitchen. The most surprising things made her feel
good, she thought later. Imagine feeling great because
her mother was going to help her with the canteen!
What a change that was!

Chapter 13

IT was like old times having Santha and Ravi back in the house for the week end. A few minutes after they arrived Tory told Santha that she had to see her new room. Excitedly, she led her up the stairs and flung open the door, her eyes watching Santha's face intently.

"Oh, Tory," Santha gasped. "It's so completely different! I have to get used to it!"

"Do you like it?" Tory asked anxiously, following Santha's eyes around the room. She had carried out her own ideas as far as she could: the bed was now free of a frame and stood neatly encased in a black corduroy spread, heaped with white pillows and two bright red ones. She had plain white curtains at the windows and a black shag rug in front of her bed. Since she couldn't paint the bureau, she had changed the old-fashioned handles on it to modern ones of square brass. The beribboned lampshade was gone and a simple parchment one took its place.

"It's stunning," Santha said, after she had taken everything in. "It's really stunning," she repeated. "It looks like you."

"What do you mean?" Tory asked delightedly.

"I don't know. . . ." Santha looked around the room thoughtfully. "It's direct, the way you are; it doesn't hide behind any curlicues. It's bold and—forthright, is that the right word?"

"I wouldn't know," Tory said. "I hope so. I'm going to forget about being soft and feminine. It just isn't me."

Santha turned to her with a mischievous twinkle. "Don't be silly. With the right boy you will be soft and feminine, don't worry! You're not the same all the time, no one is. The women in my country are fighting for their independence now, the way your suffragettes did, but when they are with their husbands they are still soft and meek and feminine. You can be both."

Tory laughed. "Well, perhaps."

But even though Tory no longer cared about being soft and feminine, she still wanted to feel passionate and involved. She wanted the private, excited awareness she had felt for Adam. Would she ever feel that way about him again? Although they were friends now, she didn't know. She had been so busy working on the dance and selling tickets to it that there had been little time to think of anything except her necessary school-work. Tonight at the dance, with Adam beside her, she would know the answer.

At five o'clock the Darling household was gay with everyone's preparations for the dance. Even Mr. Darling and Ethan were going to this one, since no one wanted to miss the drawing for the trip.

Tory and Santha took their time getting dressed. As Tory said, they were a "mutual admiration society," each telling the other how gorgeous she looked. Tory herself was pleased with the way she looked as she gave herself a last glance before going downstairs. She had picked her dress herself, a stark white silk, cut very simply, with good lines and a low neck and back. Mrs. Darling thought the dress was too sophisticated, but Tory reminded her mother of her promise to let her develop her own taste as much as possible. Santha, she thought, looked beautiful in a sari delicately embroidered with silver thread, her dark hair shining, and long earrings dangling from her ears.

Ravi was waiting for them downstairs. His eyes went right past his sister to Tory, and he let out a low whistle. "You'll knock 'em dead, as you say," he told her, his big, dark eyes glowing with excitement. His face clouded over when Tory told him that she was leaving early for the dance with Adam, since they had a lot to do, but he brightened again when she said he could have all the dances he wanted.

In a short while Adam arrived to pick up Tory. He was shining, the way he had looked when she had glimpsed him the awful night of the school dance. But when he pinned a corsage to her dress, the memory of that horrible night seemed very far away.

At the canteen they were both too busy to pay much attention to each other. The punch had to be mixed, the orchestra met, and the flowers arranged. Tory looked around the canteen with a surge of pride. This had been a great deal her doing, and it was a job well done.

"Feeling proud of yourself?" Adam asked teasingly, as he caught her looking around the room. "You look like a mother hen with a new brood."

"What a charming comparison," Tory said with a laugh. "You make me feel so attractive."

"Oh, you know what I mean," Adam retorted. "You look gorgeous, didn't I tell you that?"

"As a matter of fact, you didn't." Tory gave him a bright smile.

"Please consider it said." Their eyes met in a long look, until Tory turned away to finish with the flowers she was arranging. It was nice to have Adam near and at ease, but she couldn't wait for the dance to begin. She wanted to hear the music playing and to glide away in his arms with her eyes closed.

At last everything was ready, and the guests started to arrive. The band struck up the first dance, and Tory was in Adam's arms. This was the moment she had been waiting for, after all the summer's agony—dancing with Adam.

She looked up and met his eyes, and they smiled at each other. His face was within inches of hers; she could feel his arms around her. The band was playing their favorite song, and Tory closed her eyes. . . .

But nothing happened. Tory couldn't believe that her heart was beating calmly, that no thunder or lightning shook her. She opened her eyes and looked at Adam again anxiously. He was the same. She liked him very much, they were friends now—but the tension was gone, the magic had vanished.

Tory held on to him as he whirled her around. He said something that made her laugh, and they laughed together. But Tory's head was clear, and she felt no exciting, inner turmoil; that wonderful, mysterious, unknown something that used to send shivers through her when Adam was near was no longer there. He would never affect her that way again. He was very nice, and she liked him very much—but there it was. Finis to one part of her life.

She felt no pang when Ravi cut in on Adam, and she watched him make a beeline for Liz and cut in on her partner. As the dance went on, she didn't have much time to think about herself, but she had an odd feeling that was partly relief and partly sadness. Her mother would probably describe it as growing pains, she thought ruefully. If this was what one had to go through, it was certainly confusing. How could she look at a boy at one time and feel as if she were hitting the skies, and at another time, dance in his arms and feel nothing? Was everything going to be cut and dried from now on, with all the so-called childish magic gone?

Tory went from one partner to another. It was a good dance, with everyone eager to know who would win the exciting trip to India. But Tory was preoccupied with what she had to do. She was thinking it must almost be time to have the long intermission for the drawing, when she suddenly looked up into the eyes of the boy she was dancing with, Jack Durham, a friend of Amy's Woodie. He was down from college for the week end, and Woodie had just introduced him to Tory. Unexpectedly Tory felt her heart flutter at the look in Jack's eyes.

"Your thoughts seem very far away," he said.

"Not really. I was thinking it should be time for the intermission soon. Then we'll draw for the trip," she told him.

"Do you want to go to India?" Jack asked.

Tory's eyes were thoughtful. "Yes and no," she said. "I don't know. . . ."

"I hope you don't go." Jack maneuvered her around the dance floor expertly. "I'd—well, skip it. I hope you stay here." He said it simply, and Tory felt her heart turn over as their eyes met again.

Jack Durham—she must ask Amy all about him. Suddenly the music sounded gayer, she forgot about her duties, and the sadness was gone.

She and Jack were sitting and talking when Amy came over and spoke to her. Tory came to with a start. "Hey, it's time for the intermission," Amy said. "Everyone's waiting for the big event of the evening!"

Tory went over to the band. The drums beat for attention, and she got up on the stage with the huge box that had all the names in it. She asked Ravi and Santha to come up onto the stage with her, and she introduced them to the audience. Tory described the trip, and Ravi spoke on behalf of his family, saying how much a visit from two young Americans would mean to them. He also spoke about his country and some of the things the two guests might see.

Tory's eyes roamed around the audience while Ravi was speaking. She couldn't believe that this was all true —that the canteen was in existence, that she was chairman of it, and that they would be sending two visitors to India. She caught Adam's eye and then her mother's for reassurance.

Jack was standing up front directly facing her, and she could feel his eyes on her. She wanted to laugh at the beautiful absurdity of life, and the magnificent unexpectedness of it!

When Ravi finished speaking, Tory called a young girl up from the audience to put her hand in the box and draw out two names. Everyone waited breathlessly. The girl handed one slip of paper to Tory. She read out the name—Helen Fisher—and everyone applauded wildly. When they finally stopped, Tory read the other name—a boy, Tommy Higgins, who was a sophomore in the high school.

The place went wild with excitement as everyone tried to congratulate Helen and Tommy at once. Tory saw her mother coming directly toward her. "Tory dear." Her mother spoke in a low voice amidst all the noise. "I suppose you'll never forgive me for making you do this. I was almost wishing you had won!"

"I couldn't win," Tory said.

"Why, you had as much of a chance as anyone," Mrs. Darling said indignantly.

"Not really," Tory said with a slow smile. "I didn't put my name in the box."

Mrs. Darling's face was astonished. "You didn't? But why? I never heard of such a thing!"

Tory shrugged. "I thought it wouldn't look right if I did win—after all the fuss about my wanting to go. Maybe I'll get to India someday anyway."

There was no time for her mother to answer, because Jack was tugging her arm and pulling her away. Tory looked back and smiled at her mother.

Mrs. Darling's eyes followed her, and Tory saw a look of pride in them that made her hold her head up high. "Isn't this a wonderful world?" she said to Jack spontaneously.

"It certainly is," he agreed. "Remarkable," he added, as he took her in his arms for the next dance.